Town of
Willow Hollow
Mrs. Crawley's house
Mr. Gaunt's house
Church/ School
Pastor Stuart's house
Livery
Ben's Blacksmith Shop
General Store/ Feed and seed
Lena's house
Cumberland River

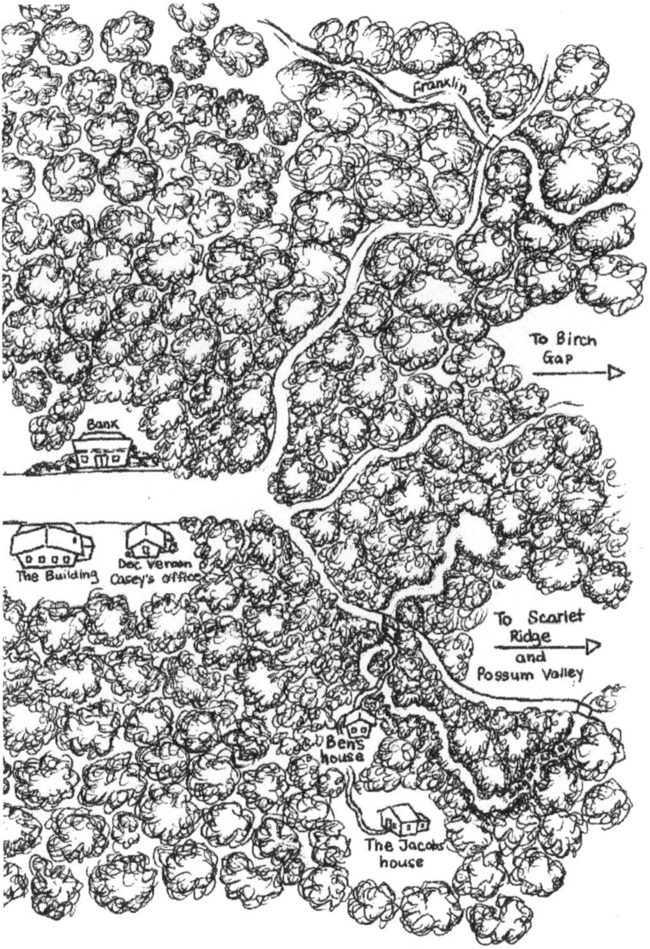
Franklin Creek
To Birch Gap
Bank
The Building
Doc Vernon
Casey's office
To Scarlet Ridge and Possum Valley
Ben's house
The Jacobs house

# The Secret Place of Thunder

*A Librarians of Willow Hollow Novella*

ALICIA G. RUGGIERI

All content copyright © 2020 Alicia G. Ruggieri.
http://www.aliciagruggieri.com
All rights reserved. No part of this publication may be reproduced in any form without written permission from the author, except for brief quotes used for review purposes.

Cover design by Amanda Tero,
www.amandatero.com.
Images from www.pixabay.com and www.depositphotos.com. Used by permission.

Willow Hollow map copyright 2020 by Elisabeth Grothjan, SparrowandRoseDesigns@gmail.com. Used by permission.

All Scripture quotations are taken from the King James Version. The author has taken the liberty of capitalizing pronouns referring to God.

All hymns used in the text are in the public domain.

This is a work of fiction. While every effort has been made to ensure general historical authenticity, all names, incidents, events, and characters are products of the author's imagination and should not be construed as real. For more information, please see the Historical Note. Thank you!

ISBN: 978-1-948171-06-9 (softcover)
ISBN: 978-1-948171-07-6 (e-book)

# Books by Alicia G. Ruggieri

*Stand-alone Novels*

*The Secret Place of Thunder (part of* Librarians of Willow Hollow*)*
*A Holy Passion: A Novel of David Brainerd and Jerusha Edwards*
*The House of Mercy*

*A Time of Grace*

*The Fragrance of Geraniums*
*All Our Empty Places*
*A Love to Come Home To*

*A Legacy of Grace*

*Each Perfect Gift*

*Children's and Family Fiction*

*Mr. Portly Finds a Purpose*
*Jemima Sudbury and the Mystery of the Missing Cufflinks*

*Other Books in The Librarians of Willow Hollow*

*A Strand of Hope* by Amanda Tero
*I Love to Tell the Story* by Faith Blum
*Hearts on Lonely Mountain* by A.M. Heath

www.aliciagruggieri.com

*You called in trouble, and I delivered you;
I answered you in the secret place of thunder...*

Psalm 81:7a

# 1

## Monday, March 9, 1936

*Why can't anyone in this backwoods place ever arrive anywhere on time?* Edna Sue O'Connell adjusted the small spectacles resting on the bridge of her nose and sighed silently. Beside her – with sufficient distance between them to assure the head librarian that she harbored absolutely no amorous intentions toward him – Curt Armstrong checked his watch again.

*It's ten seconds later than the last time you checked.* Edna shook her head and glanced across the table to where her fellow horseback librarians Lillian and Lena sat in companionable silence – Lena, of course, with her nose hidden in a book. Edna squinted and read the title on the spine of Lena's book: *Black Beauty*.

*Oh, that would be a good one to bring to the McGilliver girl.* She picked up her pencil and marked the title down in her notebook. After a pause, she decided to keep writing a list of similar books she could think of:

*Caddie Woodlawn*
*Little House in the Big Woods*
*National Velvet*

A piece of Edna's nutmeg hair slipped out of one of the twists that rolled together into a small bun at the nape of her neck. Irritation rose inside her as she whisked it behind her ear. *When is the new girl going to arrive?* A pile of books intended for Edna's patrons already rose before her. She'd chosen and stacked them by size before any of the other librarians had gotten there. Though at least Lena and Lillian hadn't been late!

*That's it.* She scribbled a final time in her notebook and clapped it shut before turning to Curt. "How long are we going to wait for her?" She let a little of her impatient scorn show, knowing it would intimidate him.

Curt lifted his shoulders in a sheepish shrug.

*Why must he be apologetic? He's a man; he has power to go and do whatever he wants.* Curt moved up on Edna's list of men she couldn't respect.

"I'm sure she'll be along any moment," he offered.

Edna narrowed her eyes. Why was he making excuses for this newcomer? "Isn't she staying here at the Building?" she asked, referring to the large single-story structure that housed the town's bathhouse, rooms-for-rent, and the Pack Horse Library.

Curt scratched behind his ear, a tell-tale sign that she'd succeeded at least in making him nervous. "She'll be along in just a moment, I'm sure."

He hadn't answered her question, which meant that, yes, this new librarian had no excuse for being late. *For making me late!* The thought pressed down on her mind, threatening to cripple her as she recalled the many chores that awaited her arrival back home. Hopefully, Molly the mule wouldn't decide to become lame again on the way back to Scarlet Ridge. She had no time for that.

*She probably will.* The irritation made its way out to Edna's fingers as she began to tap her pencil against the notebook's cover.

Curt darted a glance at her, then let his eyes settle on Lillian and Lena, both so meek and poised. "She's a delightful gal, and I'm sure you'll be as impressed as I am with her."

*I doubt that.* It didn't take much to impress Curt – not if a woman had a pretty smile and a flattering word for him. "If she ever arrives," Edna replied aloud. "Which seems doubtful." *Maybe she went back to the city while the going was good. If she has any sense at all, that's what she'd do.*

"I'm sure she'll be along any moment."

Across from her, Lillian and Lena nodded their agreement. They would – Lillian the do-gooder, who never had an evil word to speak of anyone, and Lena, who would agree with anything Curt said just to keep her job – poor little mouse, beaten down by her alcoholic mother. Edna summoned all of her willpower and stopped herself from rolling her eyes.

Well, she wasn't about to wait for Little Miss City-Girl to decide she'd had enough beauty sleep… or whatever she was doing. With a final tap to her notebook cover, Edna prepared to rise to her feet.

But the door burst open just then and revealed the new librarian.

*What in the world?* "Good grief. It's Shirley Temple." The words left Edna's mouth before she realized she'd spoken them aloud.

But no one's attention perched on Edna Sue, that was for sure. Instead, everyone in the room had joined in staring at the newcomer, whose smile radiated from her delicately-flushed face. The young woman gave a little bounce as she surged into the room, making her forget-me-not-blue dress flutter.

Edna let her eyes slide over to Curt, whose admiration for the newcomer shone. He nearly stumbled to his feet in his rush to get to her side. "I-I'd like you to meet our new librarian."

*Oh, for heaven's sake.* You'd think that he'd never seen a woman with curled hair before! Edna hardened her face into a glare and brushed away imaginary dust from her mud-brown riding trousers. *Men.*

"Ladies, this here is Miss Ivory Bledsoe. She's come to us from around Nashville." Curt said that last bit as though it should make them all hold her in the same esteem he evidently did.

Edna raised her eyebrows. Miss Ivory Bledsoe and her white-blond curls might hail from a cosmopolitan city, but her highness certainly didn't possess much sense at all if she had decided to come to Willow Hollow, Kentucky, of her own free will. *What I wouldn't give to get back to New York.* The thought alone was enough to press tears to the back of Edna's eyes. Gritting her teeth, she flipped open her notebook again and forced herself to read through the list she'd begun to make there. That would keep her emotions firmly in check.

The blond chit chattered on about how beautiful the mountains were – *Sure, and deadly, too; just look at my father* – and how no one should live without a good friend and a book – *if you can get anyone around here to read, let alone give you the time of day without shooting at you.* Of course, Lillian had to encourage her. "I'm new here myself, and, I agree, it's lovely. It reminds me a lot of my home, but warmer."

Edna looked up to find the two rose-colored-glasses-wearing young women smiling at one another. Oh, for pete's sake. She scanned Ivory from head-to-toe before sending a glance at Curt. She was unable – and unwilling – to keep the contemptuous humor from her eyes and voice. "Are you sending her out on the trail? What's she going to w–"

But, for once, Curt actually interrupted her. He laid a hand on Ivory's shoulder again. "She'll stay here with me. That is, uh, she has a place working in the library with me."

*Of course she does.* It wasn't worth Edna's while to ask why, if Curt really needed the help, he'd not advertised locally. *Ivory won't last a week.*

"I brought hundreds of new books with me."

So that was what was inside the boxes resting near the wall. Edna couldn't resist a glance over at them. Her heart hungered to open them now, but she wouldn't show Ivory how eager she was, as if they were dependent on the generosity of this flatlander.

"I'm going to help get the library organized and be here to

help recommend books to your patrons from the new selection."

*If you can get them to come to the library in the first place.* Edna had to practically beg the mountain folk to take the books she hand-delivered to them on horseback – that is, er, on muleback, in her case. This city girl thought they'd take books from a foreigner – and not only take them, but actually walk into the library and ask for her advice? As she listened to Curt introduce Lillian and Lena, a smile pulled at Edna's lips. *This I'd like to see.*

Finishing his introductions, Curt pointed at her, and Edna hid a grimace. "Now this here is Miss Edna Sue O'Connell. She's a local girl."

"Woman."

Curt frowned at her, obviously puzzled. "Huh? What's that?"

She'd been through this before with him. "I'm an adult. I'm a local *woman* – well, by extraction, at least." *Not really. And I won't be forever, either.* Even to her, though, that promise sounded meaningless nowadays. Even if she could get back to NYC by some miracle, what jobs now waited in the aftermath of the Crash of '29? And she certainly couldn't expect help from her grandmother any more…

Curt still appeared perplexed with Edna's explanation, but it didn't matter because Shirley Temple charged around the table until she was at least a foot closer to Edna than Edna was comfortable with. "I'm pleased as punch to meet you!"

The easiest thing was to play it like she was completely unaffected and disinterested. That usually turned away nosy, shallow-friendship-seeking folks. "So I see." Edna tapped her pencil against her notebook and eyed Ivory. Perhaps that would deflate this young woman enough to escape her continuing notice.

But Ivory was more determined that most. She actually moved to wrap her rosy arms around her! Everything inside Edna froze. The only thing she could think of to do was to turn away, as if she didn't see Ivory, and face Curt. From the corner of her eye, she watched Ivory hesitate and then, dropping her arms, settle into the chair beside her.

Relief replaced the tension that had filled Edna, but, just to be on the safe side, she moved her chair a smidgen more away from Ivory.

Curt shuffled the papers before him. Good. Maybe that meant that they could finally begin the monthly meeting that should have started – Edna angled her head to peek at Curt's watch – twenty minutes ago. "Well, the big news is," Curt began, "we're expanding. With the new books Ivory – that is, dear Miss Bledsoe has brought us, we have enough material to open a new delivery area."

As Lillian and Lena murmured their satisfaction, Edna glanced at Ivory. *But I thought he said that she wasn't going out on a route?* She could just picture Ivory knee-deep in mud!

Curt unfolded his map of Willow Hollow's routes. "We're going to take on new territory in Possum Valley, and I want you to see to it, Edna."

She tried to keep the surprise from her face but knew she was unsuccessful. She adjusted her position in her chair to try to disguise it. "Will I need to give up my Sugar Creek territory?" The routes included in the Sugar Creek area ran from Willow Hollow all the way up to her family's tiny farm on Scarlet Ridge. *If he thinks I'm going to switch my route and go out of my way...*

But Curt was shaking his head. "No, I want you to take on Possum Valley in addition to Sugar Creek. Of course," he added, "your salary will be increased as well with the additional area."

For the first time that day, Edna's heart lightened. Money... Money meant freedom. "By how much?" she asked, not caring if she sounded blunt. That was her way, after all; she had a reputation to maintain.

Curt appeared slightly taken aback, but he turned his eyes

down to the papers before him. "Uh, let me see if I have the figure here…"

She couldn't keep her booted foot from tapping.

"Here it is." Curt held the paper up in triumph, though his smile was directed toward Ivory, rather than Edna, the one he was addressing. "By fifty percent. So that would be an additional $14.00 a month."

*So I'd earn $42.00 altogether every single month.* She swallowed. And Daddy and Ruthie never need know that she was earning that extra $14.00. That she was tucking it away for her own future – her future outside Willow Hollow. She looked down at her hand gripping the pencil. How much older it looked than it had when she'd left the mountains for New York City twelve years ago, only to be recalled to Willow Hollow by duty just a few years later. *If my future still exists.* Which was doubtful. She'd barely finished her education, hardly obtained her teaching certificate, when the fateful letter from her stepmother Ruthie had come… and broken all her dreams into smithereens.

"Would…Would that be okay?"

Edna jerked up her head to see Curt waiting for her answer. *Pull yourself together, Edna.* "Yes, that's satisfactory."

Curt went on about how the Horseback Librarian program had decided to open a new library in Steven's Gap and how he'd be splitting his time between there and Willow Hollow, but Edna only tuned in with one ear. *With money put away, would it be possible… in time… for me to leave? Even if Daddy still lives? I could hire a nurse… Of course, I would have to save every penny…*

A commotion at the door broke through her thoughts, and she snapped her attention to the boy rushing into the room. She knew the scrappy little thing well; he was one of the only people she'd be loathe to leave behind in these mountains.

"Miss Ivory, Miss Ivory, I'm ready for my story!"

*Miss Ivory?* Edna looked from young Gerrit Callon to

smiling Ivory Bledsoe.

Gerrit seemed to finally notice that he'd burst into the middle of a meeting. He scrambled up onto the chair beside Ivory. "Oh, do I get to be one of 'em book fellas again, too?"

Curt started to shake his head, but Ivory gave the child a wink. "Of course you can, if you promise to be as quiet as a mouse."

Edna couldn't help the smile that twisted up her lips as Curt visibly pouted but said nothing. *Jealous of a child, Mr. Armstrong?* How ridiculous.

"See there, Edna? I'm a bookman, just like you is a bookwoman!"

With a grin splitting Gerrit's face in half, Edna couldn't help but return his smile. A softness that she both feared and loved fell over her heart at the sight of his sweet innocence, and she returned her attention to her notebook, listening as the conversation continued without her.

"Is Edna your friend, too?" Ivory asked Gerrit.

"She's my cousin." There was a note of pride in his voice, like he was glad to know her. Edna bit her lip.

"Is Lillian your cousin, too?"

*Oh, heaven help us!* Figures that a born-and-bred city girl would believe all the rumors about the Kentucky Appalachians.

"I don't reckon." Gerrit eyed Lillian. "Are ya my cousin?"

Lillian chuckled in that carefree, soft way of hers. "No, but I'm staying with the Stuarts, and I believe that Mrs. Stuart might be your cousin."

"How delightful!" Ivory nearly clapped her hands.

*Is this real or put-on?* Edna couldn't help the small smirk that lifted her lips. Sometimes, it was better for her to keep her mouth shut. Most of the time, it simply wasn't worth it to say anything at all. These people – and people in general – would never change. All she could do was stay aloof and observe.

Curt cleared his throat, thankfully putting an end to the nonsense. "Now that that's settled, let's continue, shall we?"

A sigh of relief rose from her lungs. Knowing Curt, he still had a half-dozen unimportant things he wanted to talk about, and the morning was passing quickly.

# 2

Nearly an hour later, Curt dismissed the meeting. As the others turned to each other with smiles and chatter, Edna grabbed the stack of books towering in front of her, slapped her notebook down on top of it, and jabbed the pencil into her bun. Scooting back her chair, she rose to her feet swiftly. If she made it out of town by noon, she could be back at Scarlet Ridge Farm sometime in the early afternoon. She'd wait to have dinner until she arrived home – maybe grab a quick bite to eat before she tried her hand at mending the goat pen fence one more time.

But Curt strode toward her, a finger raised to let her know that he needed to speak with her. "Don't go disappearing, Edna Sue. I've more information for you about Possum Valley."

She tried to hold back her irritation, but it must have shown on her face anyway because Curt's mouth turned down. "Look, Edna, if you don't want the new area, it's all right. I just figured that you have no children, no home of your own, you see? That is, I thought maybe you'd have the time for it – and the money's sure helpful for anyone... Besides, you're the boldest gal here. But I see that I should've thought before assuming you'd want to take on something more."

*No children.* No husband, either, though she was well over thirty now. *An old maid.* Only an invalid father and a cantankerous stepmother. Oh, yes, and goats and chickens and a farm that was always in need of repair. She gritted her teeth against the unintended sting of Curt's comments.

"I suppose I could ask Lillian to take it," he went on. "She's busy, but she always manages to fit one more thing in."

The offense piled on top of the hurt of Curt's previous comment. Why in the world should Curt think that an outsider – and even after a month, Edna Sue still thought of Lillian that way – would do better at handling an additional area than she would? Before she could stop herself, her mouth opened. "I'll take it. I haven't changed my mind. You don't need to ask Lillian."

Curt raised his brows. "Are you sure? Because you don't have to take it, you know."

Edna Sue nodded. "I know." But she really did have to take it, didn't she? The extra money promised – $14.00 a month! – was the first ray of hope she'd encountered in many years. Perhaps, after all, she might escape from Willow Hollow.

"Well, all right, then." Curt rubbed his hands together; Edna couldn't blame him. This large room, while perfect for housing the local library as well as town committee meetings, reaped a heavy draft from its in-need-of-repair windows. "It's... It's a rough area that you're going into, though. I just want you to know that, off-the-bat."

She eyed him. "All of the area around Willow Hollow would be considered rough to outsiders, Mr. Armstrong. What exactly do you mean? Where do these routes go in Possum Valley?"

"Past Scarlet Ridge to the east, down Possum Valley and then up to... Well, in all honesty, the territory itself – well, it's – that is, it's not exactly mapped out yet. That's... That's part of what I need you to do, as well as deliver the books. Some of the farms – some of the dwellings – are not on any map a'tall. And those people up there... Well, they might come down to town maybe once-a-year, before the snow flies. If then." He hesitated for a moment, then went on, his voice quiet, rushed.

"It's very backward. Lots of odd characters about who aren't used to seeing outsiders."

Her mouth quirked. "Thought you just told Ivory that I'm a local woman."

He flustered. "You are. I mean, someone from outside their little gulches and ridges. Even a fellow mountain woman." He leaned a little closer, and on his breath she caught a whiff of the fried ham he must have enjoyed for breakfast at Mazy's boardinghouse table. She stepped back. "If I were you, Miss O'Connell, I'd carry a rifle."

*A rifle?* Well, as long as she had agreed to take on the new routes, she needed to put the bravest face to this. She forced a smile onto her lips and replied, "I'm sure it will be fine, Mr. Armstrong. I'm well-accustomed to taking care of myself."

"If you're sure."

"I'm quite certain, yes."

"All right. You won't need to do Possum Valley's routes more'n once a month, at least to start. If it picks up interest, then maybe we'll expand it to the regular twice-a-month rotation. Your salary would then pick up accordingly."

Her heart beat faster. *These people will be interested. I'll make them interested.* The promise of another $28.00 a month dizzied her.

After Curt had given her a few more directions, he moved off toward Ivory, of course. Lillian and Lena still were choosing new books for the patrons along their routes, so Edna had no trouble at all slipping out the door, through the entry area, and out into the noontime bustle of downtown Willow Hollow.

*Noontime bustle, my foot. Downtown?* She nearly snorted at the thought, but it was true: If she went into any one of the very few tiny businesses open along this main street, they'd tell her that she'd come at a busy time – After all, there might be another customer in the shop!

She shook her head and moved toward the General Store. She needed to pick up some liniment for her stepmother, though she was tempted to forget about it and head straight home for the chore-packed afternoon ahead of her. Just as she moved off the wooden steps, though, she remembered that she'd left her sweater hanging on a chair inside the library. Sighing, she turned to head back inside.

"Whoa!"

And with that exclamation came a collision with the person emerging from the Building at the exact time she had turned to go back inside. The impact hit so hard that it knocked the wind out her for a moment, though mercifully she kept her footing.

*Merciful?* There was nothing merciful about it!

And the books! They'd all thudded to the plank steps as she'd lost her grip on them. There they lay, some opened upside down, pages flapping. Without a thought more to whoever the knucklehead was who had collided with her, she dropped to her knees, grabbing for the copies.

"I'm terribly sorry, miss! Sometimes, I'm awfully clumsy."

She refused to even glance up as she continued picking up the books.

"Here, let me help you," said the voice above her.

"It's the least you can do!" she snapped back.

But it took him forever, it seemed to Edna, to lower himself. Irritated, she scooped up the last few copies and lifted her gaze at last to spear him through.

But then she realized why he'd taken so long.

*It's the schoolteacher.* The one with such a limp that it was noticeable from a hundred paces. Watching him for a fraction of a second longer than she'd intended, she saw that his left knee could not bend properly and that he was trying to kneel with his right knee, keeping the left leg straight. Watching him, pity softened her heart. At the unwanted sensation, she shook herself mentally and pushed the feeling deeper down, where it sank beyond her acknowledgment.

Still, in the face of his disability, it was hard for her to maintain the same level of irritation. "Don't worry about it. I have them." She rose to her feet.

He still crouched halfway to the planking, the strain evident on his face. Should she help him up? A great weariness hovered at the horizon of Edna's soul. *So much pain... so much suffering.*

Better not to help him. Better not to get involved in yet another person's pain. Didn't she have enough of her own troubles? Besides, if he didn't do it himself now, what would happen if he fell when no one was around to help him? Better not to let him feel dependent. Better not to *be* dependent, if one could help it.

"Would you mind giving me a hand?" He raised his face to smile at her. "I foolishly left my cane at home."

Her sense of duty overcame her hesitation. Holding her pile of books beneath one arm, she reached out with the other.

The schoolteacher grasped her forearm. "That's it. Just stay steady; hold your ground. On three. One. Two. Three."

He heaved himself up, and Edna felt thankful that, though his height rose a solid half-foot above her, he had a very slight build. Some would call him gaunt.

The man huffed with the effort, wheezing a little. "Hated to ask it of a woman, but that was the leverage I needed. Thank you, Miss…?"

"Why did you hate to ask it of a woman?" She knew she sounded brash; she didn't care. Obviously, this misogynist needed a little rudeness to shake up his ideology.

His brows rose above his brown eyes. "Pardon me?"

Edna maintained her stare. "I said, why did you hate to ask a woman to help you? Was it beneath your dignity to do so? A woman is good for you to look at, to wash your linens, to keep your house, but not to do you the service of helping you up from the ground?" She was going to be terribly late returning home, but she wasn't giving this one up without a fight, especially since this man was actually the one responsible for training the young minds of Willow Hollow!

He stood there, his dark lashes blinking for a few moments as he gazed down at her. Awkwardness stole over Edna Sue, though she tried to repel it. A little smile quirked up the man's lips.

She opened her mouth. Did he find her amusing? She would straighten that out. She was no toy to be played with, no object to be laughed at...

"You misunderstand me, miss," he said at last before she could rail against him once more. "It was for the sake of your own higher dignity that I wished to spare you the burden of helping one whose delightful duty should be to assist you, should you require it."

His words – both what he said and how he said it – drove the sharp words from her own tongue.

After a moment, the man's smile grew. "I'm Cecil Gaunt. I've seen you around town; I know that you work for the Pack Horse Library program, is that right? But I'm afraid I don't know your name."

She nearly smiled at his name, given what she'd recently thought about the man's build. Well, what could it hurt to let the man know her name? That would not break any of the barriers she'd set in place to keep her from being hurt by those nearest to her. Edna raised her chin and looked Cecil in the eyes. "I'm Edna Sue O'Connell. And yes," she added, holding up the stack of re-gathered books, "I'm a librarian with the WPA program." She held out her hand to shake his, knowing that as an obviously-polite man, he would not offer his to a lady first, even in this modern age.

His hand, smooth and small, met hers with a firm but gentle grip. "Very pleased to make your acquaintance at last, Miss O'Connell. I've been meaning to get over to the library, but school is usually in session during your open hours. We're having our dinner break right now."

"Oh? You like to read?" She raised her eyebrows. Most men around Willow Hollow did not care to read, even if they knew how to. Most of the male schoolteachers – including the one who'd been in charge of Willow Hollow's school when she was a girl – thought that the most important subject to teach was mathematics – what they called *ciphering*.

"Yes, I don't know how I'd live without a good book by my side. 'The person, be it gentleman or lady, who has not pleasure in a good novel, must be intolerably stupid,'" he added with a grin.

So, he could quote Jane Austen. Still, skepticism niggled at her. "I'm surprised you haven't made more of an effort to come to the library, then. From what I recall, the school has precious few books. You must enjoy a great deal of re-reading?"

There came that soft smile again. "I do, but I also have my own personal library, Miss O'Connell. I wish to visit the town library for the sake of my students. As you say, the school's collection is seriously lacking." He gestured toward the stack Edna held. "And I see that the town library has gathered some more current literature. I know that those would encourage the youngsters to read outside of their schoolwork – *Anne of Green Gables*, *Little House on the Prairie*. I even spy Edith Nesbit there in your hands. Reading will open these children up to the possibilities that God may have for them outside the mountains as well as here in them."

Despite his unnecessary reference to God, Edna permitted her estimation of the schoolteacher to rise. *At least there's one person who actually enjoys reading in this place! And who thinks of possibilities outside these imprisoning mountains.* "Well, I have to be on my way. Excuse me."

He tipped his hat. "Good afternoon, Miss O'Connell. Delighted to have met you at last."

*Afternoon?!* Mumbling a reply, Edna hurried off. She still had to visit the store for that liniment! And sure enough, the sun had risen well overhead. *Confounded Ivory Bledsoe and her lateness! Confounded Curt Armstrong and his puppy-love for anything pretty!*

At least Edna need not worry that Curt would ever direct his ardor toward her. In her mid-thirties, she was well-past what most mountain-folk considered the prime of a woman's life; in fact, some of the Willow Hollow women her age had a grandchild on the way. Besides, she lacked the natural sweetness a man liked. *Good thing, anyway.* A man would just get in the way of her plans… if her plans ever panned out.

It was only when she was on her way out of town that she remembered that she'd forgotten to retrieve her sweater inside the Building after all.

Leaning against the Building's rail, Cecil gave his bad leg a minute of rest while he let his own eyes follow the retreating back of Miss Edna Sue O'Connell. A smile quirked at his mouth. He shook his head. Well – a lady in trousers, with a dozen books under her arm, a fiery mind, and the loveliest brown eyes he'd ever seen behind the wire-rimmed spectacles that balanced on a nose some might say was a smidgen too big for her face. Cecil didn't think it, though. In fact, if someone had been privy to his thoughts, they'd have found that Edna Sue O'Connell appeared to be exactly what Cecil had been waiting for – and hadn't even known it.

# 3

## *Wednesday, March 11, 1936*

As Edna Sue urged Molly to pick her hooves through the rocky, barely-broken path, she wondered if she had agreed to Curt's request hastily. These people deeper in the mountains probably had never met anyone who lived more than five or six miles from their homes. And she knew the kind of things these gulches and glades could harbor: mountain lions, bears, poisonous snakes – not to mention men with shotguns and stills to hide. Regardless of how she'd brushed off Curt's advice, Edna always carried a rifle; after all, the written word was not always more powerful than the sword, so to speak.

The Kentucky mountains rose around her, full of sunlight and shadow, full of loneliness and beauty. Edna had learned long ago that she could not let her mind or heart linger too long on the effect these mountains had upon her, or they would overcome her inner ramparts.

Around Molly's feet, the infant spring ferns gave way, revealing jewel-like moss beneath them. How long had it been since someone rode down this path to reach the town of Willow Hollow? Curt had given her vague directions; she knew he had never been past Scarlet Ridge himself. *Follow Sugar Creek*, had been his only real advice.

And so she did. She would follow the creek for a road, as

it had apparently been for others before her, given the rough path that ran alongside its bank. She tried not to think about next winter, when the creek would swell with frigid water, and Molly would be forced to thrash her way across – little as any mule liked that. *Though, perhaps by then, I will be gone...*

She drove the thought from her mind. For her own departure to become a possibility, something else had to happen – something she could not wish for, despite everything: Daddy's death. *I will have to keep waiting.* She gritted her teeth.

The silence settled over her as she rode. She couldn't determine how long Molly had been treading the trail – two miles? perhaps three? – when she saw a streak of color moving ahead of her. She squinted at it. Someone ran between the trees, small, moving quickly as a rabbit.

*"Lots of odd characters about who aren't used to seeing outsiders."* Curt's words came back to haunt her.

Her heart picked up its pace. She stared through her small spectacles, took a deep breath, and forced herself to call out. "Hello! Hello there! I'm from the library in Willow Hollow, and I've brought you some books to borrow."

But the person – whoever it was – melted into the thickets that shadowed the woods ahead of her. No matter how hard she squinted, she could see nothing. She braced herself and brought Molly to a complete halt. The person lingered, watching her; she could feel the invisible eyes. She swallowed back the fear that taunted her. "I'm following the creek for my road. I won't come any farther unless you tell me that it's all right."

That was the safest way. You never knew when a man might be protecting his still or when you might be mistaken for a person with whom bad blood existed.

She waited a moment more, but only silence answered her. Not even a crackle in the brambles told her whether someone yet remained. She wavered between going on – and risking her life – or accepting defeat here – for the day, at least. *Maybe they know Daddy.* Licking her dry lips, Edna Sue tried a last-ditch effort. "I'm Doctor O'Connell's daughter."

Who knew whether her father had ever made it this far afield in his work, years ago now though it would have been?

Molly shifted beneath her as she waited again. She almost had given up when, about a hundred feet off, she saw that speck again. But, this time, whoever it was didn't run away.

She squinted. She really needed new spectacles. It looked like… a little boy? Wearing blue overalls? She took his willingness to make himself vulnerable out in the open as a sign that it was all right for her to come closer. Edna Sue nudged Molly's broad sides with her heels. "Come on, girl."

Molly's sturdy legs picked their way through the brush, among the tall trees reaching their open branches towards the heavens, until they'd nearly reached the boy. The towheaded child of ten or eleven stared at her, lips straight and taut, his suspicious eyes bearing a color of which the sky should be jealous. She cleared her throat and plunged forward. "Hello, young man. I'm Edna Sue O'Connell. I'm working for the Horseback Librarian Project in Willow Hollow, and we are providing a way for you people—" She hid a wince as the boy's eyes narrowed further. Emphasizing the distinction between the mountain-folk and the town-folk or between highlanders and flatlanders – well, that was certainly the way to get off on the wrong foot here.

She tried again. "That is, I mean, we're working together here in the mountains to be able to circulate books and magazines and, oh, all sorts of reading material."

The boy, who despite the chilly weather, did not wear a coat or shoes, still stared at her, wordless. Edna Sue steeled herself against the piercing nature of those bright, unblinking eyes. She pinned a smile to her face, trying to be as warm and welcoming as she knew other librarians would be in this situation. Ones like Lillian, whom Curt had offered to put on this route in her place.

She decided to try another tactic. "Is your mama or daddy

at home?"

The boy continued eyeing her for a long moment. Then, with the same suddenness with which he'd appeared, he turned on his heel, slinging a battered rifle over his shoulder. Noticing it, Edna Sue realized that he had been patrolling his family's property, who knew for what reason. A still? A feud?

Clenching her jaw against the thoughts, she decided to take his turned back and stride away from her as an invitation to follow up to the cabin. "Come on, Molly," she said, nudging the mule again with her heels. Molly, who'd found a patch of fresh spring greens, was loathe to go on, but after a little more encouragement with Edna Sue's heel, the creature headed after the boy. Edna took note of landmarks as they went so that she'd be able to get back to Sugar Creek on her own, if need be.

"Don't need no book-learning here." As if to emphasize this, the boy's mother slammed the enormous cast-iron frying pan down on the hot stove. Edna Sue's eyes widened. The woman had lifted that with one hand; Edna Sue would have been fortunate if she could've heaved it with both of hers.

She cleared her throat and pushed out that false smile again. She would succeed at this. She would show Curt and all the other librarians – everybody – that she could force the mountain folk to accept the education they should want – for their children, if not for themselves, surely. And she would earn her extra fourteen dollars, if it killed her.

She sucked in a deep breath of herb-scented air and reminded herself that it was a small miracle that she had gotten both feet inside the door. "Mrs....?"

"Holbrook. Vergie Holbrook. My man's name be Ira."

Edna Sue offered her hand. "I'm Edna Sue O'Connell," she said, finishing the introduction she'd tried to make when she'd walked into the one-room cabin. "And, as your son said,

I'm with the Pack Horse Librarian program that the Works Progress Administration has started down in Willow Hollow, among many other towns."

"Towns." Mrs. Holbrook glanced at Edna's extended hand but didn't move to meet it with her own. "Don't need no fool books." She reached above the stove for a cannister, its label peeled-off, reached in two meaty fingers, and scooped out a hearty chunk of lard. With a practiced fling, she let it fly from her fingers into the pan on the stove, where it sizzled with enthusiasm.

Edna glanced at her surroundings: curling newspapers insulating the walls, yellowed by tobacco smoke, three small children, all apparently under the age of five, rolling around on the floor, alternately laughing, playing, slapping one another, and crying. Then Edna's gaze caught once more on the young boy she'd met outside, who now stood like a sentinel at the open door, his gun on his shoulder.

*This is hopeless. What am I doing here?*

But then she saw – or thought that she saw, at least – a flicker of interest lighting up that same boy's eyes, hidden behind the wariness and weariness. The flicker gave her courage.

Edna turned back to the boy's mother and cleared her throat. "But what's wrong with books, Mrs. Holbrook?" Edna asked in what she hoped was a convincing tone.

Mrs. Holbrook turned toward the table, whisked the covering off a giant bowl there, and gave a mighty punch to the risen dough inside. Edna held back a wince in sympathy for the dough. The woman rested her hands, red and calloused, deep inside the floury folds of the large lump. "What's wrong with book-learning?" she repeated Edna Sue's question. "It'll take him away from the hills, that's what. He'll abandon his own kin and kith, all for the sake of a few worthless words on a printed page. It's what m' brother Ossie done."

Edna Sue felt at a loss. She knew that what Mrs. Holbrook

said was true. Those who received an education often did turn from the mountains that had birthed them, often did go into the city, leaving their roots. *Daddy did.*

But he had returned to these hills in the end. These mountains possessed the strength to shackle their people forever. Or some people, at least. "You don't know that for sure," Edna Sue replied, knowing the words must sound weak in the ears of a woman who had someone dear to her walk out of her life, probably never to return.

From the corner of her eye, Edna Sue caught a movement. An older girl, maybe twelve or so, who had been quietly sweeping all the time Edna had been in the cabin, put aside her broom. Now, she peeked inside the saddlebags that Edna Sue had draped over the single kitchen chair. As usual, Edna had jam-packed the bags with books. She decided to change her tactic.

"Not all of the books are meant for education, you know, Mrs. Holbrook. Some of them are meant to keep children busy – out of mischief. I have picture books, magazines. Books to entertain children, you see."

Mrs. Holbrook stopped her kneading one more time and looked her straight in the eye. "You mean, books that'll take 'em away from their chores?"

Edna felt her face heat with exasperation. "No, no, that's not at all what I mean."

Mrs. Holbrook grunted and turned back to the stove. Without flinching, she slid salted ham slices into the popping grease.

Edna pressed on. "Of course you wouldn't want your children to be taken away from their chores. But occasionally, you must want a little time to yourself… yet the children keep crying for your attention?"

As if to set himself up as an example, the youngest child who lolled on the floor received a heavy slap from one of his playmates and began bawling – a high-pitched cry that encouraged Edna to invest in ear-plugs.

Mrs. Holbrook released the heavy sigh of a woman who knew no rest, day or night. She surveyed her squalling brood for a moment before stepping over to the supposed perpetrator and thumping him on the back of the head.

"Yow!" The victim of the thump added his own screech to that of the youngest.

"Time for m'self?" the woman questioned Edna Sue with a humorless cackle. "Sure, I'd like a little of that."

Edna quickly stepped over to the saddlebags. The girl who'd been peering inside spooked away from them. What Edna wouldn't give to be able to scrub the child's grubby face and hands clean!

She pulled out one of the two picture books that she had brought along, both added to the library recently by Ivory. "Look, here's the kind of book I'm speaking of. *The Poky Little Puppy*. Nothing harmful in that."

One of the small children from the floor, a girl with strawberry-blonde curls straggling down her back, edged her way up to Edna Sue's elbow. Edna tilted the book so the little girl could get a better look at the cover. The girl's eyes implored Mrs. Holbrook.

Edna Sue held her breath as the mother looked from the book to the girl. Then her gaze – eyes the same sky-blue as those of her sentinel son – narrowed in on Edna. "What'd you say your back name was again?"

"O'Connell. My front name's Edna Sue," she offered, purposefully using the colloquialism.

"And you're Doc O'Connell's gal?"

"Yes, ma'am."

The woman pursed her lips. "Your daddy gived some medicine to my man years ago now, when he took powerful sick."

"Oh? And did he recover?" Edna Sue held her breath.

The woman gave a single nod. "Yep. I was much ableeged

*The Secret Place of Thunder*

to your daddy, Miss Edna Sue. Don't know what I'a done without Ira around and a passel of young'uns crawling 'round my toes. 'Course, weren't as many then. Young'uns, I mean."

Edna was relieved to know Mrs. Holbrook's number of toes had not lessened in the intervening years.

Mrs. Holbrook took the book from Edna and eyed it silently for a few heartbeats. Even the children on the floor quieted, as if knowing that something momentous was about to take place. "Well, all right. I reckon one book can't hurt. I'll trade ya… some strawberry jam from last year's crop. How 'bout that?"

Edna Sue limited herself to a small smile and nod. Victory had never tasted so sweet.

---

"Won't take none of your lit'rature, as you call it. Stuff o' the devil, I say." The dark-haired woman picked up her straw broom and whacked the rag rug that hung over her porch railing. A cloud of dust rose, and Edna Sue coughed into her elbow.

"But there are Bible storybooks, Mrs. McCabe. And Sunday School booklets," Edna Sue wheedled. Never on her usual Sugar Creek routes were people so resolved to dismiss the opportunity for books!

The woman snorted and narrowed her eyes. Behind her, Edna Sue caught sight of a tiny child peeking out the door of the dark, windowless cabin. The little girl's big eyes swept Edna's Sue heart into them, like quicksand.

She blinked back the emotion that threatened to cause her to plead with Mrs. McCabe. *Emotion gets you nowhere. Base your actions on the facts.* There were many children just like this one who would never see a storybook; why should she care about this little girl? Would her compassion matter? *No.* Better to just get down to business: earning her fourteen dollars. If Mrs. McCabe wouldn't take the book, Edna Sue would have to ride on to the next farm.

If this ramshackle place could truly be called a farm. Edna Sue glanced to the side as the scrawniest chicken she'd ever seen – alive, at least – picked its way through the muddy remains of what she assumed was last year's attempt at a vegetable garden. She'd seen no other animals. *What do they live on?*

"Mrs. McCabe—" she began again.

But the woman interrupted her. "I'll thank ya kindly to git off my property. Like I said, we don't need none o' your tomfool books."

"But Mama—" The whisper pleaded from the doorway.

"Get inside, Pearl!" Mrs. McCabe snapped. The child dissolved into the cabin's darkness. When the woman turned back to Edna Sue, a snarl twisted her lips. "Now, you listen up real good. My man's out right now, or you might've a bullet-hole in your gullet for coming here without an invitation. Now, I said it nicely once – git – and I won't say it so nice next time."

Indignation burned a trail through Edna Sue's body, but what else could she do?

She got.

---

*How much farther can I go?* She'd been following the creek for at least a solid mile past the McCabe place, she estimated, and had come across a neglected graveyard, wild thickets that promised blackberries come summertime, and several winter-hungry deer cropping on the twinges of green that peeked through the mud.

But no people to read the books she carried.

These new routes had to succeed. They *had* to. If they did, Curt had promised that she'd receive a full salary for it, just as she did for her usual delivery area. Fourteen dollars was good; twenty-eight was better. *Especially if I want...*

She closed her eyes and then opened them, staring straight

ahead into the greening trees. *Focus.* No time to dream about what the future might bring. Better simply to take advantage of this opportunity and see if it might, just might, lead her out of this mountain prison in which she'd been kept for a decade.

Around the bend of the creek, her patience met its reward: Ahead, the chimney of a rickety cabin coughed a trail of smoke. "Whoa, there, Molly." Molly gladly obliged her, dipping her head to sample a little of the bright green grass.

"Hello!" she called out at the top of her voice. "My name is Edna Sue O'Connell. I'm here with the Pack Horse Librarian Program from Willow Hollow."

Hearing no rifle clicking, she assumed it might be safe to dismount. She edged her way off Molly and slung the reins into a slip-knot over a low-hanging branch nearby. "I've come to see if you'd like to borrow some books or magazines," she continued in the same loud voice, eyeing the cabin ahead, knowing that an unseen someone most likely looked out the single window at her. The window had no glass; greased paper covered it, but a rip in that paper would permit an eye to spy out whoever approached.

As she neared the cabin, she couldn't help but shake her head at the sad state of neglect. *How can they live like this?* A tree punctuated the front porch, growing straight through the floorboards and up through the rotten roof! *Lazy and backward!*

As she tested the weight-bearing ability of the porch with her foot, the door creaked open a few inches. A white-frosted head poked out. "W-Who's there?" A tobacco-stained gray beard muffled the words; the apparent toothlessness of the speaker further garbled them.

Edna Sue registered the vacancy of the man's gaze. *Blind.* She tried to ignore the guilty recollection of her earlier thoughts about the tenants' laziness. "My name is Edna Sue O'Connell. I'm with the Pack Horse Library program down in Willow Hollow."

The man squinted, as if trying to focus on what she said.

After a moment, he muttered, "Cain't rightly understand ya. My ears ain't working too good no more. But ya voice don't sound dangerous. Female, ain'tcha?"

Edna Sue leaned toward him. "Yes!" she fairly yelled into his ear.

The man gave a satisfied nod. "Thought so." He opened the door a little wider and turned to go back inside. "Come along into the house. Mary'll be right gladsome to have a bit o' female company. All she's got now is this ol' crackerjack." He chuckled as he shuffled inside. "Mary! Ya got yourself a vis'tor! Wants to swap howdies with ya."

# 4

The sun had gone past its zenith when Edna Sue mounted Molly again, her saddlebag just as full as it had been when she'd arrived at the ramshackle abode. Mary Hansen, it had turned out, might not have been as hard-of-hearing as her husband Dag, but she proved to be just as blind. True, the old woman – hands crippled by arthritis, nearly chair-bound – had delighted in Edna Sue's company, but Edna left with discouragement slumping her shoulders. What good was an elderly couple's welcome if they wouldn't be regular borrowers on her route? Despite that, however, she'd reluctantly agreed to the Hansens' insistence that she stop by the next time she rode this way.

While Molly bent her long neck to slurp the water of the ice-cold creek, Edna hesitated over whether she should continue farther upstream or if she should turn back for the day. She surely didn't want to be stuck out here in the dark, not only because Daddy and Ruthie would expect her to return, but also because the Kentucky wilderness held many dangers at night – even more than it did during the day. Her rifle would protect her only so far. Still, the Hansens had told Edna that several families lived throughout the miles around their cabin, and the thought of some success tempted her to keep going.

Undecided, she opted to think it over as she ate her noon

dinner astride Molly, rather than dismounting and potentially encountering snakes sunning themselves on the creek bed. Removing the leather string from the mouth of her dinner sack, she munched her jelly sandwich, as well as a handful of last autumn's walnuts, already cracked open so she could eat them easily as she rode. Swallowing the last bite of bread and jelly, she made her decision; she'd go farther. Opportunity never came to those who sat on their heels, afraid of the dark.

As she continued to ride uphill, she thought over the folks whom she had encountered thus far along this route. Though she'd spent much of her own life in the Appalachians, she'd never seen such poverty as this. These people were far removed from even the mostly-defunct coal-mining towns. They lived far, too, from the towns such as Willow Hollow, which might have provided at least part-time work or the opportunity to sell goods. Instead, many of these hill people lived off their stills and whatever sparse vegetation they could coax from the thin Kentucky topsoil. Edna Sue despised the way her heart sank as she'd surveyed the haunted eyes of the children, the broken-down women, the men ruined by alcoholism, the crippled and abandoned elderly.

*Hope deferred makes the heart sick.* The Scripture, spoken long ago by her mother's lips, haunted her mind. Edna dismissed it, her spirit twitching in anger. True though it was, what did it matter? There was nothing to be done about it. These people had always lived like this; probably always would. *There's nothing I can do about it. Better to not even care.*

Just look at where caring had gotten Daddy and Mother: one, struck down to a shell of the man he'd once been; the other, six feet beneath the soil.

After having stopped at a few more homesteads, she eyed the sun. Though her descent down the mountain would take much less time, she wanted to be certain that she would reach home before dusk. "Come on, Molly. Let's head back. This is far enough for today at least." She lifted her reins to turn the mule when she heard something.

The barking of a dog. She hesitated. *Someone's home must be near.* She fingered her saddlebags. She still had two books left: a tattered Bible commentary, which some well-meaning city minister must have donated, and a copy of Milton's *Paradise Lost*.

*There is really no point in going on. They won't want one of these books, anyway, I'm sure.* Who up here in this backwards country would? When she could get them to accept a book, they preferred colorful magazines, recipe books, children's stories, and maybe something like *Tom Sawyer*, occasionally. A Bible commentary and a tome from the seventeenth century? Probably not.

But even as she decided to turn back, a black-and-white creature flashed between the trees ahead of her.

The shaggy little mutt rushed toward Molly and began to bark again, wagging its feathery tail. Gratitude toward the old mule rose in Edna's heart as Molly stood, solid as a stone statue, unmoved by the dog's antics. Edna eyed the dog, hearing friendliness in its bark. She reached inside her saddlebag for the crust of jam sandwich she'd tucked into it.

"Here you go." She tossed the piece of bread. The dog caught it in midair, springing off its hind legs, light as a deer. It swallowed and stared at her, ears perked expectantly.

She felt her first smile of the day—first real one, anyway—rise to her lips. "Oh, so you're my friend now, are you?" She nudged Molly forward with her heels. "Well, take me to your master or mistress, then."

Edna Sue could have sworn that the dog frowned at the lack of more jelly-and-bread coming its way. "Well, off with you," she urged, planning to follow the dog.

But the mutt began barking again, and this time Molly began to shift uneasily beneath Edna. "Whoa, there! It's all right," she calmed the mule, but even she could hear the nervousness that crept into her voice. The little dog danced beneath the mule, barking louder than she would have given it credit for, due to its petite size.

After several seconds of this, Molly had enough. With a snort, the mule took off at a trot, heedless of Edna's command to stop. The dog, delighted with this turn of events, took off after the mule. Molly's trot morphed into a gallop.

Galloping on a mule that had taken its own lead, Edna Sue found, was not a comforting thing—especially after she dropped the reins. They dangled, whipping around the mule's flying feet, as the odd threesome bolted across the meadow toward the trees. Edna Sue hung onto the saddle's horn with white fingers.

In those moments, she was even tempted to pray.

They shot past the line of trees and burst through a huddle of budding bushes into a clearing. Edna had barely enough time to glimpse the cabin that hunched there before Molly came to a rather sudden stop.

Edna Sue did not.

When she opened her eyes, blue sky met her gaze, pounding filled her head, and a warm tongue slurped her face.

She groaned and turned her head a smidgen to see the culprit's moist black nose within inches of her own. The dog even had the nerve to wear a worried expression!

She turned her head to the other side and saw Molly, now quite content, munching a little new grass nearby. After testing her limbs one at a time to see if she'd broken anything, Edna rose to her feet. The dog jumped up, putting its paws on her now-muddy trousers. She pursed her lips and then gave it a little pat. It wasn't the dog's fault that it was untrained and unattended.

*I'm going to find this dog's owner and give him a piece of my mind. Keeping a dog wild and untrained! Uneducated mountain people – He's probably just like his dog, but not as nice!*

"Hello! Is anyone here?" She revolved slowly, taking in

her surroundings: a south-facing vegetable garden which had already been turned over for spring planting, a three-sided shelter, and a small moveable chicken coop. The small cabin nearby appeared to have been erected in recent years—odd indeed for this area of the mountains, where many folks had roots that traveled back to the eighteenth century. *Odd. Very odd.*

A shiver ran down Edna's spine. She had no idea who lived up here. It could be anyone. It could be someone... well, dangerous. Perhaps, perhaps, just this once, she should let it go. Turning to Molly, she reached for the reins, preparing to mount again.

But then she saw a movement behind the cabin, where the trees melted into shadows.

She gritted her teeth against fear. "Hello?" Her voice sounded weak even to her own ears. Frightened. She tried again. "Hello! Is... Is anybody here?"

The dog took a final sniff of Molly's hooves and then, woofing again, loped off towards the back of the cabin. Edna forced her feet to follow into the cool darkness of the trees.

"Hello? I know that someone's here. I... I'm a librarian with the Pack Horse Project. You're on our new route, and—"

Behind her, a gun clicked. She swallowed against the panic that choked her.

"Please remove yourself from my land." A low, smooth voice spoke very calmly into the pine-scented air. Inch-by-inch, Edna Sue turned.

A middle-aged man, his clothing hanging on his thin body as if pinned to a clothesline, stood a few feet away. His gun pointed straight at her, held by only one arm, the butt tucked into his armpit. The other shirtsleeve folded against his body—empty of its usual occupant. A wild and frazzled beard swathed the lower half of the man's face, matched by the overgrown gray thatching his head.

"I said, please remove yourself from my land, miss."

Edna Sue's fear gave way to rage. "You have the audacity to tell me to get off your land, sir? When your dog nearly chased me to my death? And now you dare to threaten me with a rifle! How can you—"

To her astonishment, a peal of laughter rolled out of the ruffian's throat. His eyes, hard and dark as polished black stones, lit with amusement. Edna couldn't prevent her jaw from dropping open as the man, continuing to chuckle, lowered his gun and turned on his heel, striding off toward the cabin.

He was *laughing*... at her! The weariness and discouragement of the day rolled to a boil. She'd had more than enough of these ignorant highlanders. Steps stiff with indignation, Edna marched after him, heedless now of the gun he swung by his side.

"You might find me amusing, sir, but I find *you* both crude and coarse. I'm part of the Pack Horse Library program, though I'm sure that someone like you wouldn't be interested in that. Of course, you of all people are the most in need of its benefits. Perhaps reading a book occasionally might teach you a few lessons in being a decent human being. It just might refine your mind, temper, and personality, all in one go! You should try it sometime!"

In her fury, Edna realized that she'd followed the man around the cabin to the front steps. He placed his hand on the railing and turned, settling his eyes on her.

They were calm now—filled with neither that inscrutable hardness nor with the gaiety he'd enjoyed at her expense. They looked deeply into her, as though they sought to draw the water from her very soul. He raised his eyebrows. "Are you quite finished, miss?" he asked.

Uncomfortable in the scrutiny, she realized that she had no more words. She gave him a single nod and turned to go back to Molly.

She had one foot in the stirrup when the librarian in her guilted her into turning back to him once more.

He still stood, facing her, one hand on the railing, that foolish black-and-white dog peeking out from behind him.

"Would you... Would you care to try a book?" she offered stiffly, the ire she still harbored lingering in her tone.

A corner of his mouth turned up. "I don't need your books, miss. But I thank you."

She fought against rolling her eyes. He was just like everyone else in these mountains—content with mediocrity, not even willing to take hold of the hand offered to them to help them rise above their circumstances. "Why should you not even *try* a book? Even if you can't read, there are pictures..." She then thought of the two books – the Bible commentary and Milton – left in her saddlebags. "In most of them, anyway."

"Miss, I don't need your books," he repeated, his smile now turning up the other corner of his mouth.

"But if you would just—"

"*Je n'ai pas besoin des livres.*"

For the second time since encountering this man, Edna Sue felt her jaw drop open. During her schooling in New York, she'd learned enough French to realize he'd answered her in that language.

"*Nolo libros.*"

And in Latin.

"*Ich will die Bücher nicht.*"

That *had* to be German, didn't it?

"*Antio sas.*" With one last smile, he strode up the steps and into the cabin, the black-and-white mutt at his heels. The door shut behind him.

*What in the world?* Edna stared at the closed door for a long moment before turning to Molly and swinging her sore body into the saddle for the long ride home to Scarlet Ridge.

# 5

She'd made Molly trot most of the way home, eager to arrive before the sun slipped behind the mountains. Dusk came earlier to the mountains than it did in the flatlands; dawn, too, came later.

The familiar sight of Daddy's farm bowed her shoulders. A lot of work still awaited her. Gritting her teeth, she straightened her back and dismounted. She led Molly into the small paddock attached to the ramshackle animal shed. The mule stood gratefully as Edna removed its bridle and saddle. She slung the saddlebags over the fence; she'd retrieve them once she'd finished her work out here. Molly moved over to the trough while Edna heaved the saddle into her arms, slinging the bridle over her shoulder, and headed into the shed. Her muscles already ached from the fall she'd taken in Possum Valley. She dreaded to think of what she'd feel like, come morning.

Inside the shed, Edna placed the saddle over the sawhorse and hung the bridle on its hook. She eyed a bale of hay near the door, ready to feed to the goats and Molly. How tempting it was to collapse onto it! *If you do, it'll only be more difficult to get going again.* She took her own advice and headed back out into the crisp spring night, an old curry comb in one hand, a bucket of grain in the other.

Molly's ears pricked up at the sound of the rattling grain, as did the ears of the three goats in the smaller pen nearby. "I'll get to you in a minute," she told the goats.

*I really must be going crazy from living here in these mountains – I'm talking to goats now.* What would Grandmother think, or Edna's old city beau, Theodore? Quickly, she turned her mind from pondering questions that didn't need to be answered. She put down the bucket for Molly and worked quickly to curry the sweat and dirt out of the mule's coat while the animal ate its supper. Putting aside the curry comb, she retrieved a handful of clean straw and used it to brush away the accumulated dirt and sweat. A gentle pat finished the job, and Edna led Molly into the shed to her loose box.

Her own stomach gnawing her insides, Edna retrieved another few scoops of grain and led the goats one-by-one to the milking stand. Their mouths busy, she milked each of the nannies. Finishing with them, she let them have free roam of the shed.

*Almost done. Keep going.* She clenched her teeth and pushed herself off the milking stool, heading outside to lock the chickens into their coop for the night. In the morning, she would gather their eggs as well as milk the goats again.

At last, she turned toward the cabin. Only a dozen yards lay between it and the barnyard, and Edna Sue took them slowly, though her stomach ached with hunger and goosebumps rose on her arms. This time of night always pulled her in such different directions. One half of her longed to run from that little cabin, far away, never to return; the other half yearned for the crippled man who sat inside, aching to connect with him once more. If only she could…

She pulled a deep breath into her lungs. It sounded ragged against the soft night that settled its wings over the murmuring mountain world. Pushing her shoulders back, she let herself glance once more northeast—toward the city from whence Daddy, Mother, and she had once come so long ago now—

before taking the well-worn path to the cabin door.

The scent of soup greeted her as she unlatched the door and pushed it open. Her stepmother Ruthie turned from the stove with a bare nod. Her eyes adjusting to the lamplight, Edna Sue peered toward where her father usually sat. Sure enough, there he dozed. His arms hung slack over the sides of the chair, his head tilted back, resting against the handcarved headrest. His mouth hung open an inch, letting the saliva drip down, unwiped. His legs, skinny from disuse, flopped out before him, utterly lax.

As she did every night, Edna turned away, her heart gripped in a vice of pain and anger, once again conflicted between the love she felt for Daddy and the repulsion that gripped her.

"How has he been today?" she asked Ruthie, setting down the saddlebags by the door. She removed her hat and coat and hung them on a peg near the door.

Ruthie shrugged, a potato rotating in her hands as she peeled it. "Same as usual, I s'pose."

*Why do I even ask?* Nodding, Edna stepped over to the washbasin to scrub her hands, though she knew that Ruthie didn't care whether she did so or not, before joining her stepmother in peeling potatoes at the table.

A few of the lines in Ruthie's stony face relaxed. She set down her knife and the potato and wiped her hands on her ragged apron, heavily soiled from days of use. "Take over for me, will ya, Edna Sue?" She hobbled away from the stove. "My rheumatism's a-hurtin' today somethin' fierce." With a groan, Ruthie sank down onto the rocking chair that companioned the one in which Daddy sat.

Without responding, Edna Sue continued to peel the potatoes. *Is it any wonder that I sometimes feel like Cinderella?* Except there was no Prince Charming hovering nearby. *Not that I desire one.*

Ruthie's voice cut across the room. "Where did ya go

today? Thought this was your day off from that fool book thing."

Edna Sue's heart lifted in rebellion. "It usually is, but Mr. Armstrong wishes me to ride other routes occasionally, in addition to my usual ones."

Ruthie sniffed. "Hope he's a-paying you well for that. We need ya 'round the house, ya know. I can't lift your daddy myself."

Edna Sue had decided from the get-go that Ruthie didn't need to be told anything about how much she would be paid for taking on Possum Valley. At any rate, none of that money would go to support Ruthie and Daddy; her regular Scarlet Ridge routes – which she rode on Tuesdays and Thursdays – already did that. Possum Valley's payment would be all hers, kept for when she could finally shake free of this place. She stayed silent, hoping that Ruthie didn't seek an answer.

"I don't know why they bother with all this Pack Horse Library stuff, anyway," Ruthie went on after a moment. Though her rheumatism was acting up, her tongue certainly knew its full capability tonight. "It's not as if the people up here in these hills care about books and learning. It's a lot of long-headed nonsense, iffen you ask me."

*But no one did ask you, did they? Though you had no problem with long-headedness when you thought my father was your lucky break twenty years ago, did you?* She held herself back from speaking aloud. She'd done so before, and the results made the effort worthless.

"My work does bring in twenty-eight dollars a month," Edna Sue reminded Ruthie. Had her stepmother forgotten that the Pack Horse Project provided their only sure source of cash income? The goat's milk and farmer's cheese could be traded for credit at the general store, but rarely did they see any real money come from it.

Ruthie seemed to chew over that one a little. "Yeah, well, there's that, I s'ppose."

A smug smile pulled at Edna Sue's lips. No matter how much Ruthie grumbled about the way the pack horse work took Edna Sue away from the farm anywhere from two to four days a week, her stepmother never complained about the money that the work brought in. And one mention of that was usually enough to quiet her other grumblings.

Edna Sue took advantage of the silence that stretched between them to ask something that had been weighing on her mind for the past few hours. "Do you know the man who lives on the far side of Possum Valley? He has a little black-and-white dog, seems to live alone."

The rocking chair squeaked as Ruthie moved back-and-forth. "Possum Valley, you say?"

"Yes. I didn't see any evidence of farming, except for a small vegetable garden and a few chickens. The cabin seemed to have been built in recent years, too. And he… he's missing an arm."

The squeaking stopped. "Don't you go near that man."

At the sharpness in her stepmother's tone, Edna Sue paused, her knife halfway through the potato peel. She didn't turn around. "Why?"

"That man's got God's curse on him; I'm sure of it. He brings it on everybody who comes near, too. You listen up, girl. I done lived long enough in these mountains. When I tell you not to go near Henry Ravenhill, you don't go near him, you hear?"

"Yes, I hear you, Ruthie." But that didn't mean she had to agree, did it? Or obey, for that matter. She was a grown woman, for heaven's sake. Slicing the last of the skin from the potato, she began chunking it into the simmering pot of soup, taking care to avoid splashing the broth. *So his name is Henry Ravenhill.*

Hours later, after she'd spoon-fed Daddy some of the

potato soup, after she'd swept the kitchen, after she'd helped Daddy get into his nightclothes, Edna climbed the stairs to the loft and dropped down onto her own pallet-style bed. Too tired to bother changing into her own nightgown, she lay flat on her back, staring up at the rows of onions and garlic hanging from the rafters. They made an odd kind of starry vegetation.

*How did my life become like this?* Every night, the same question rolled through her mind. Though she knew the answers, she continually felt stupefied by the way her life—by the way she herself—had turned out.

As a seven-year-old child, growing up under the roof of a privileged New York family, she would never have guessed that her father and mother hovered on the verge of returning to Daddy's roots in the Kentucky Appalachians – the calling of a God whom Edna Sue would soon learn to mistrust.

At Scarlet Ridge, the farm her doctor-father carved out of the earth during his rare free time, ten-year-old Edna Sue could not have imagined the tragedy that the year would hold: the death of Mother through a mysterious illness that Daddy tried to cure in vain.

Then, thirteen-year-old Edna Sue, still grieving Mother's death in a desperate, childlike way, had not anticipated that Daddy would return home one day with a mountain woman he said would become her new mother: Ruthie, who seemed as bewildered by Edna as Edna was by her.

At seventeen, Edna could not have predicted the letter that would arrive from Mother's mother, her grandmother, still back in New York… bidding Edna to return to the city and become all she had been born to be: schooling, parties, beautiful clothing, and more awaited her. Daddy, seeing the disintegration of his home through the constant squabbling between Ruthie and Edna, had finally agreed.

Yet, only five years later, Edna also had not foreseen the arrival of another letter—just as she'd accepted Theodore, too. The missive demanded that she return to the mountains once more, this time to care for Daddy, whose brutal workload had incurred a stroke.

A stroke that turned out to be irreversible and with worse effects than she'd imagined. When she had arrived back at Scarlet Ridge, Edna knew that her life as she knew it—her escape from these terrible mountains—had ended. Daddy and Ruthie's refusal to relocate to the city confirmed it. Then, when she didn't return to her grandmother's home, she'd received a courteous letter from her fiancé, letting her know that she could keep the diamond ring if she wished, but there would be no gold band joining it.

Had that life—her life—ended forever? Now, turning on her side and seeing through the floorboards the flicker of lamplight in the room below, she supposed that, yes, perhaps it had. For her only escape from Scarlet Ridge now was Daddy's death, and…she couldn't wish for that. No matter how much she still felt angry with him, she couldn't wish him dead.

# 6

It was just plain foolishness to suggest that the man was under a divine curse of some kind. "More mountain superstition!" Edna Sue declared aloud to Molly as she headed down the Ridge into Willow Hollow a few days later.

"Now I wonder what you'd do if Molly answered you." The familiar male voice startled her, and she whipped toward the bushy area from which it had come.

A man with a gingery head of tousled hair parted the bushes. He didn't smile, but a friendly expression shone from his kind eyes.

"Benjamin Thrasher! Don't you know that you can scare a person to death, creeping in those bushes like a snake?"

Ben raised his eyebrows. "But snakes don't talk, cousin. Leastways, not since Eden."

She pursed her lips, trying to prevent a smile from creeping onto her lips. "I have no time for your foolishness." Rolling her eyes, she nudged Molly into a walk, but then a thought popped into her mind. The son of Daddy's long-dead sister, Ben had lived near Willow Hollow all his life; he'd be just the person to ask about the one-armed man living near Possum Valley. Besides, Ben didn't possess a superstitious bone in his body... unlike Ruthie. She tugged back on the reins, bringing Molly to a halt.

"Say, Ben," she began.

Her cousin had already begun striding away, but her voice called him to turn. "Yeah?"

"Do you know the man who lives way up in Possum Valley?"

Ben raised his brows again and gave a low whistle. "Didn't know you librarians went all the way up yonder."

She shook her head. "I just started a new route there. Mr. Armstrong told me I could carve my own path. I've been following Sugar Creek all the way."

Ben stayed quiet, thinking, and Edna felt her patience trickling away. "Do you know him, Ben? I have to get on with my day, and—"

He held up a hand. "Hold your horses, Edna. There's a lot of men up in Possum Valley. Which one do you mean?" He eyed her. "And if you're going all that way by yourself, you'd best have a rifle with you. There are some real unsavory characters up thataway."

Edna placed a hand to the gun strapped behind her saddle. "I am carrying one." Goodness, didn't anyone in Willow Hollow think that an independent woman of a certain age could take care of herself? "The man has one arm." That should be description enough; she hadn't come across many folks in all her life with one arm, except for a few lingering Civil War veterans when she was still a girl.

Ben was quiet so long this time that Edna Sue had already opened her mouth to tell him never to mind, when he finally spoke again. "That's Henry Ravenhill. I've cut wood for him a time or two. Delivered it up there." He shook his head. "You ain't got nothing to be afraid of from Ravenhill."

Now it was Edna's turn to raise her eyebrows. "No? He aimed his rifle right at me."

Mirth shadowed Ben's expression. Edna grew indignant. "I don't think it's funny at all, Ben. And his dog nearly ate me." Well, all right, that was an exaggeration, but still... she had fallen right off Molly!

Now Ben actually snorted. "His gun ain't loaded, Edna. Never is. And that dog wouldn't hurt a flea that bit 'er, so I can't say I rightly believe you on that score."

Not loaded? No wonder Ravenhill had laughed his way back to his front door! "What in the world was he doing waving it around at me, then?"

"Were you trespassing?"

"I…" Edna Sue hesitated. "My *job* is to trespass. I have to if I'm going to bring light to those trapped in the darkness of these mountains."

Ben lifted an eyebrow. "Thought that was Jesus Christ's job, Edna. Or are ya working for Him now?"

She scowled. "Certainly not. You know my opinion on that nonsense." Daddy'd worked for Jesus Christ, as Ben put it, and look where it had gotten their family.

"Too bad. I would've been glad if you'd answered differently this time." He turned to walk away.

"Wait!"

Ben faced her again. "Yeah?"

She squirmed inside. She hated being at the mercy of someone else when she needed anything, even information. "Why… How did he come by his education?"

Ben quirked his head like the parrot Edna Sue's New York City grandmother owned.

"Ravenhill spoke to me in three or four different languages," she explained.

He narrowed his eyes. "Why are you so curious? You ain't usually one for gossip."

She bristled. "I'm not after gossip, Ben Thrasher. Mr. Ravenhill simply is a client on my route. But I see you'll be no help."

Without another word, she turned Molly around and headed toward town. The sound of her cousin's quiet guffawing egged her into a brisk trot.

53

Leave it to uneducated Ben Thrasher to think she was funny! And where was her little cousin Gerrit, Ben's ward, while he was off galivanting through the woods? How like a man – his head in the clouds, not caring what became of the nephew he'd taken in when the boy's parents died a year ago – more lives these mountains had snuffed out too soon.

Her uncharitable thoughts irritated her. Ben wasn't really like that, she had to begrudgingly admit to herself. He did want the best for Gerrit... though, in Willow Hollow, the "best" was dismally lacking, to Edna Sue's thinking anyway.

The postage-stamp-sized town of Willow Hollow opened before her as she emerged from the woods, and she heard the school bell ringing. Recess must be over; Mr. Gaunt would be standing at the schoolhouse door, waiting for each child to return to the terribly inadequate hall of learning.

*But at least they have something.* The children in Possum Valley had nothing – absolutely nothing. She clenched her teeth as she remembered the hunger in that McCabe girl's eyes – hunger not for physical food but for some kind of mental stimulation. *Why shouldn't she have a chance at a different life? A life outside these horrible mountains?* Sure, Edna Sue brought books – though some of their parents didn't even want those – but what about everything else? Math and science, real literature. *Those children need a school, too.*

As she turned onto Main Street, her eyes found the schoolhouse. Sure enough, Cecil Gaunt leaned on his cane at the top of the school steps as the last child skipped inside. His gaze found hers as he turned. A smile rose on his lips, and he lifted his hand in greeting.

She hesitated a moment. Oh, what harm could it do to be friendly? Especially with someone who actually could read a sentence without falling asleep, if he'd spoken the truth to her? She lifted a hand and gave a brief wave.

And then an idea popped into her head.

She brought several pounds of goat cheese to the General Store, as well as eggs. The storekeeper, Walter Clark, added the value of the goods to her account, and Edna had the pleasure of knowing that she could secretly put away even more of her income, saving for that day when she might escape these mountains, just as she hoped the children on her routes could. The money on her family's General Store account meant that, each time Ruthie asked Edna to purchase something, she could use that credit, rather than her hard-earned cash.

Coming out of the store, she glanced at the sun and then the school building. An hour or so remained before school let out for the day. She'd go to the library first and gather her ammunition.

---

The school building's warmth welcomed Edna Sue. She'd waited until she saw the last student burst from the doors before marching across the schoolyard, past the crudely-built seesaw and baseball diamond marked out with burlap sacks of sand. Now, she held the door so that it would close silently behind her, straightened her sweater, and brushed a dirt mark off her trousers. She'd given up trying to look feminine and pretty years ago, when she'd been recalled to these God-forsaken mountains. *Not God-forsaken,* she corrected herself. *Cursed by His presence, rather.* The presence of the Almighty hung heavily here. Blessed were those who could escape both the mountains and Him.

"Hello? Is someone there?" Mr. Gaunt called out from beyond the coatroom area.

Edna raised her eyebrows. He must have the hearing of a jackrabbit. "Yes, it's me."

The tap-tap of a cane met her ears. "And who's 'me'?"

Humor touched his voice as he approached the coatroom.

It was a pleasant voice – disarming even her a bit with its genuine kindness. Edna Sue hurried out of the cloakroom and into the schoolroom. She hated being cornered. "Edna Sue O'Connell." She offered a hand. "We met a few days ago, outside the Building, if you recall."

His smile grew, and he met her hand with a gentle, firm shake. "Of course. I'm delighted to see you again, Miss O'Connell. What brings you to the schoolhouse?"

His friendliness unnerved her a little, though she couldn't put her finger on why. "I… I came to bring you some books for your students. You said that you're not able to come often to the library during open hours." She opened the satchel she'd slung across her torso and pulled out a few of the books she'd selected – her ammunition. "*Rebecca of Sunnybrook Farm. Tom Sawyer. The Count of Monte Cristo.*"

"How very kind of you." He took them from her as if the volumes held treasures. "My students – well, some of them – will greatly appreciate this. And I will be sure to tell them to keep the books in good condition. I certainly appreciate this."

Edna Sue nodded, her tongue knotted. How should she bring up her plan to him? She'd never worked together with anyone very well, and she'd always felt ill-at-ease making light conversation, easing her way into things. She bit her lip. Perhaps she should just go…

"I wonder, would you care to come to my home for tea, Miss O'Connell?"

# 7

The teacups clinked as Cecil placed them on the small tray. From her place on the worn but comfortable chair near the window, Edna Sue took the opportunity her host's busyness afforded her to glance around his tiny house, located behind the school. It held just two rooms – the one in which she sat at his two-person table and in which he had an efficient little kitchen set up and another beyond, its open door showing her the footboard of a bed. Like most houses in Willow Hollow, the lavatory stood out-of-doors and the school board had not installed either running water or electricity. The house was spotless and utterly tidy, not at all what Edna Sue would have expected from a backwoods bachelor.

"Give me a moment more, and we'll be ready," Cecil assured her.

She pulled her eyes away from her perusal of her surroundings to see that he had pulled the kettle off the wood-burning stove and now poured steaming water into the small china pot. When he glanced up and found her eyes on him, he offered her another smile.

She returned it. "It's all right. I don't need to return home for a while yet."

He lifted the tray. "Excellent. That gives us time to talk."

*Talk? What does he want to talk about?* She stiffened.

She'd come with her own plans, but had not thought he would have some of his own.

Cecil limped his way over to where she sat. Too late, Edna Sue realized she should have taken the tray from him, as he wasn't able to lift it and use his cane, too.

But he didn't appear to hold her thoughtlessness against her. "Since I first saw you, I've wanted us to become friends."

She tried to hide the quizzical look that she knew must have appeared on her face at his statement. Why should he want to befriend her – a plain-looking spinster who had failed at making anything of herself? *Not failed, really, from my own accord – forced to fail by the will of God.* If it had not been for His interference, she could have made something of herself; she was certain of it.

Cecil poured tea for them both, and as he lifted the amber liquid to his lips, she plunged forward. "Why is there no school past Scarlet Ridge – in the Possum Valley area?"

Cecil paused a moment at her question. Then he took a small sip of tea, placed his cup back into its saucer, and sighed. "Five years ago, before I came to Willow Hollow, the last teacher in Possum Valley left due to the mission organization's lack of funding. He was never replaced."

"Well, can't the parents pay for a teacher, all together, as we do in Willow Hollow?" Even as she asked the question, Edna Sue knew how foolish it sounded to anyone who knew the poverty of Possum Valley – and its attitude toward education of any kind except that which had to do with the inside of a whisky bottle.

Sure enough, Cecil smiled knowingly. "You know as well as I do, Miss O'Connell, that most of the folks up past Scarlet Ridge don't have an interest in schooling of any kind. I doubt any of them would contribute so much as a penny to making their children become 'long-headed', as they call it. Even in town, I am confronted with resistance constantly."

She shook her head. "It's so…frustrating! These stubborn

hill-folk." Her outburst warmed her with embarrassment, and she lifted her teacup to her lips to distract herself.

When she raised her eyes, she found Cecil's mild gaze on her. "May I ask, Miss O'Connell, why you are so interested in the children gaining an education?"

"It would enable them to escape these awful mountains." The explanation slipped past her lips, unfiltered, and she tensed for just a moment, knowing that most inhabitants would take offense at her insinuation. They didn't want to escape and thought little of those who did. *But why should I care whether Cecil approves or not?* She lifted defiant eyes to meet his gaze.

But his expression held no censure. He offered her a soft smile. "There's nothing terrible about these mountains. Perhaps, if I might be so bold as to suggest it, you could learn to see them through different eyes, as I do."

She frowned. "What do you mean?"

He fingered the handle of his teacup. "Maybe the ugliness is not in the mountains. Maybe it is in us."

She shook her head. "How can you suggest that, Mr. Gaunt? Life is so… hard here." Hard didn't even begin to describe it. In her mind, she saw Mother's grave, freshly-dug; she saw Daddy returning home with her stepmother for the first time; she saw the telegram that told of how Daddy had suffered a stroke – all offenses brought by these hills and their unfeeling God – beautiful, yes, but so terrible.

"Yes, life is hard here. I won't disagree with you on that score."

She leaned forward. "So would you not agree that education is the only hope for these children? The only hope for getting away from the hardness they experience here?"

He looked at her again with that mild expression. "Hardship is not always something to escape from, Miss O'Connell. It's often a tool in the hands of the Almighty. If only we could let Him use it to shape us into the people He wants us to become!"

She held back the bitter laughter that scummed to the surface. "What does He want us to become, Mr. Gaunt? Broken-down, ignorant, whiskey-guzzling fools? Because that's what the majority of these children – no, all of them – will become as a result of the hardships they endure here. Better to take them away from the mountains."

Her breath came fast with emotion as she finished. Etiquette tempted her to apologize for the brazen way she'd answered him, but she repulsed the urge. She raised her chin. Surely, the schoolteacher would show her to the door now; no longer would he crave the friendship with her that he said he'd desired.

Yet Cecil did not. Instead, he sat there, his face dancing with thought, his eyes on his half-full teacup. "Is that what I am to you? I'm a child of these mountains."

For the first time in a long while, heat rushed into her face. "Of course not! Of course not, Mr. Gaunt. That isn't what I meant."

After a moment, he rose to his feet and limped heavily across the front of the room to the other window. From the sill, he lifted a small tomato plant, rooted in a blue bowl with a chipped rim. He shuffle-limped his way back to her, bowl cradled in his hands.

Edna Sue moved the tea-tray to the side, and Cecil deposited the tender plant on the table between them. Easing himself back into his chair, he fixed his eyes on the plant. "Pastor Stuart's wife gave me this plant when it was a seedling, a month or so ago. She knows how much I love tomato-and-mayonnaise sandwiches in the summertime, and she thought that I'd like to have my own source of tomatoes."

Was this his way of changing the subject? Of getting out of an awkward conversation in which they didn't agree? Edna knew that many people didn't like to debate or hash out areas of disagreement. But avoidance had never been her way, and it had cost her a lot of would-be friends over the years when she'd pursued a debate at any cost. Well, what was one more? "Mr. Gaunt, I—"

He held up his hand. "Let me continue, Miss O'Connell." The smile had returned to his face, and surprise awoke in Edna when she realized that stubborn grit undergirded his voice. *Hmph.* And she had thought him passive and pathetic.

Well, she would let him have his say. "Go ahead. I'm listening."

He nodded his appreciation. "Thank you. Now, this tomato plant. If I had put it outside on the day Mrs. Stuart gave it to me, hoping it would thrive and produce, what would have happened?"

She couldn't help the smile that rose to her own lips. "The teacher in you is coming out, Mr. Gaunt."

His eyes twinkled. "I suppose you're correct, Miss O'Connell. Will you humor me and play the student?"

She paused, feeling constrained at the thought of voluntarily putting herself in someone else's power, however trivial. "Very well," she finally acquiesced.

"Well, then, what would have happened?"

"The plant would have died. It couldn't have taken the harsh weather we've had, especially since it began its life so protected, indoors."

Cecil nodded. "Yes, you're right. If I had placed my tomato plant out-of-doors from the get-go, well, I wouldn't have a tomato plant any longer, would I have?"

She shook her head. "But I fail to see how this relates to…"

"Patience, Miss O'Connell. I will explain my reasoning. More tea?" He lifted the pot.

"No, thank you."

Filling his own cup once more, Cecil took a sip. "You said that life is hard here. I agree. But we disagree on this – on whether the hardship is good or evil. You believe it is an evil, best escaped. I believe it can be used for good, great good, if endured in submission to God. You see, this plant is weak because it has been sheltered. And it needed to be sheltered – It needed to be started indoors – if I wanted to get early tomatoes from it. Now, however, because it has been sheltered, because I wanted to get the largest crop possible from it, as early as I could, I must care diligently for the plant. I cannot just set it outside, despite the weather being just right for tomato plants now – no chance of frost. I must acclimate it – I must *harden* it – by setting it outside and letting it endure the cool days and nights for a few hours at a time, bringing it inside at times so that it can adjust slowly. There is good that comes from sheltering, as I will gain early tomatoes from the plant, Lord willing. Yet, this plant is also more likely to wither in the face of harsh weather until it acclimates." He pushed himself up from his chair. "Will you come with me outside?"

"All right." Curious, Edna Sue rose from her own chair and followed him through his back door.

He limped his way across the yard toward the brambly bushes that ringed it. "Do you see there?"

She looked intently to where he pointed with his finger. "Another tomato plant."

"Yes. A wild one. I didn't plant that one. And, given the choice, I wouldn't have chosen to plant it here in the thicket, where it will have to struggle for its fair share of necessary sunlight and water. But it is planted here. Though it must endure hardship, it is able to persevere through that hardship far better than the coddled plant I have on my windowsill. It may not bear tomatoes as early as the one inside may, but it may prove to be a hardier plant in both the long and short run."

He turned from the thickets, and Edna fell in step with him as he limped back toward the house. "You wish to give the children ease, Miss O'Connell, so that they can achieve good things in this life. I don't believe that your desire is a bad one; you wish them well."

"I want to give them hope." *Something I have lost for*

*myself.*

He stopped, wincing a little as he took the weight off his bad leg. "Hope," he repeated. "For this life only? Hope of a little happiness in the things that can be taken away from us with the snap of a finger?"

*A snap of the Almighty's finger, that is.* Did God laugh as He smote those who did His work? Like Daddy?

"That kind of hope doesn't have a foundation, Miss O'Connell, if I may be so bold as to tell you my mind. But if we can give these mountain people – all people, really – the ability to persevere in hope no matter what life throws at them – like this wild tomato plant does, that really would be worthwhile, wouldn't it?"

*No matter what life throws at them.* She gritted her teeth against the memories of the years of pain these mountains had inflicted on her, against the way they had made her lose all hope – except the hope of escape. "That's impossible," she stated. "Hope can always be lost." *Hasn't even Daddy lost his hope?*

But Cecil had the nerve to shake his head. "No, I know that it's possible to possess an eternal hope. I have experienced it for myself. I grew up in Beaver Gap, not far from here. As a boy, I was afflicted with polio."

She'd wondered at how his leg had become crippled. Her heart softened at the few words, but immediately she raised a barrier to distance herself. She had known too much pain herself; how could she relieve someone else's hurts? How could she bear to sympathize when her own infected wounds merely wore scabs, not scars? "Everyone has difficulties," she stated to show how unaffected she was by what she took to be the lead-in to a sob-story.

He tilted his head. "I'm not looking for your sympathy, Miss O'Connell. I'm telling you that, through the years of sorrow and disappointment I suffered, I have come to understand deep within my soul that hope is not found in something, but in Someone."

"What?" Now he spoke nonsense. She'd expected more from a schoolteacher, obviously somehow educated outside these mountains.

"Hope is only found in Jesus Christ, Miss O'Connell. Not in physical wholeness, not in worldly success and achievement, not in moral accomplishments, not in education. God can use all these things, yes, but real hope is found only in Jesus Christ, in His righteousness. It's in Him alone that we can find peace and rest—"

"I have to go." She shook her head, trying to clear it of the things Mr. Gaunt had spoken – things that hurt as they echoed against the walls of the past and present. "I need to get home. Excuse me."

Not caring if he thought her rude, Edna Sue left without another word or glance.

---

She heard Daddy coughing as she approached the cabin that night, and dread filled her heart. Her feet stopped on the path. She closed her eyes against the twilight splendor of Scarlet Ridge and wondered if she could simply run away, never to return.

*But you know you can't.* Something drew her to that man inside the cabin as surely as the eagles sought the treetops. Was it love? Hate? *I don't know anymore.* A numbness spread over her. She squared her shoulders and pushed open the door.

Ruthie sat in her rocker, pale and worn; Daddy's chair was empty. Edna glanced toward the bed. Sure enough, Daddy huddled beneath the blankets, a shivering pile of bones and skin. She forced herself to go to his side, move away the blanket from his face, and touch his brow. He turned his head a little but kept his eyes closed, as if exhausted.

"How long has he been like this?" she asked.

"Since this morning," Ruthie snapped out. "Iffen you'd stay at home like ya should, maybe you'd a-knowed that."

"I had things to do in town today." Edna Sue decided not to mention the cheese and butter she'd brought to the store. Ruthie would think they could afford more supplies next time she went to town. "And Daddy seemed fine when I left."

"Well, he ain't fine now, as you can see. Got a real bad cough. Had a time of it a-getting him into bed by m'self."

Edna looked back just in time to see Ruthie scowl at her. *If I wasn't bringing in money and working the farm, where exactly do you think you'd be?* She restrained herself from speaking the thought aloud; doing it would bring nothing but further strife to her already-ugly relationship with her stepmother.

"Come on, Daddy, let's get you to sit up a little."

"He's too sick to sit up."

She spared a glare for Ruthie. "If he doesn't sit up, the cough'll settle in his lungs. Is that what you want?"

Ruthie grunted and packed her corncob pipe with tobacco.

She tucked her hands under Daddy's armpits and, with a fair amount of effort, managed to prop her father's nearly-limp body against the carved headboard. Edna looked away from the hearts-and-vines pattern as quickly as she could. Daddy had carved it as a wedding present for Mother many years ago.

"Do you have some soup?"

Ruthie released a puff of smoke from the pipe. "Soup? What do you reckon I am, girl? A servant? How much work do you expect me to do? Soup! She wants soup."

"I don't want your soup." Edna gritted her teeth, determined to keep the conversation as civil as possible. "I'm asking for Daddy. He could use some broth."

"Feed a cold, starve a fever," retorted Ruthie. "That's what I always say."

"Well, he has a cold – that's clear."

Ruthie pursed her lips around the pipe's stem and squinted

at Daddy. "Eh, looks mighty flushed to me. Seems to be a-burning up. Anyway, I didn't make no soup today. Too much work to do. And not enough help." She gave Edna Sue a pointed look before settling her graying head against the back of the rocker and closing her eyes.

A scream of frustration fought to escape Edna's lungs. Instead of letting it loose, she stomped across the room toward the woodburning stove. She stoked it with hands rough with anger, then filled a small pot with fermented goat's milk before clapping it onto the burner. Pulling a cannister of oatmeal from the shelf, she dropped a couple of handfuls into the pot and added a pinch of salt. "I'm going to fill the water bucket. Don't let that pot boil over. Please," she ground out.

Ruthie didn't open her eyes, but Edna knew her stepmother had heard her. Grabbing the nearly-empty bucket, she closed the door behind her, taking note of the way one of the hinges had loosened. *Have to get to that soon, too.*

Heedless of the deepening shadows, she trudged toward the pump that rose from the ground beyond the animal shed. *Maybe it would be for the best if something did happen to me.* She lifted her eyes as she approached the pump. There were mountain lions out here, and packs of coyotes, too. She'd heard them howling at night. Many locals said that coyotes wouldn't go after anything bigger than a chicken, but she knew from personal experience that a hungry animal could get desperate, and desperation could easily overcome fear. She let her imagination loose, picturing Ruthie finding her – or what was left of her, at any rate.

She let the bucket drop by the pump and kept walking toward the light that remained from the sunset, brimming over the edge of the ridge itself. Daddy and Mother had chosen this piece of land for the sunsets and for the border of maple trees that turned blood-red each autumn, earning the farm and ridge their name.

But Mother was long gone now, and Ruthie had never

cared about sunsets. Daddy could barely move from his bed to the rocker, never mind come outdoors to watch a sunset. So much around the farm still remained makeshift, left that way after Mother died and Daddy sank into a cycle of depression and overwork before his stroke.

Edna sucked in a breath of air still tainted with winter's chill. *Trapped. And I can't escape.* She hugged her arms around herself. *I can't escape from these mountains. And I can't escape...* Tears burned in her eyes, but she shook her head, unwilling to let them fall, afraid of what might happen should she do so. *I can't escape the anger that I feel toward Daddy... and the grief.* If only she could just never feel anything ever again!

She eyed the edge of the ridge. How easy it would be to take one step at a time until she reached the edge, and then... simply step over and fall... fall... fall into oblivion. *At least it would be an escape.*

Or would it? Even here – perhaps especially here – alone, at the edge of Scarlet Ridge, she sensed a Presence she could not evade. In the city, she had managed to distract herself; that was one of the things she had loved most about living there. But here, with the hills towering above her, smoky blue, pregnant with majesty, she could not escape it... Him. In one way, it brought a strange comfort – in another, a sure dread. Perhaps that was why she so rarely came to the precipice of Scarlet Ridge any more.

She eyed the edge, closed her eyes, and returned to the pump.

# 8

## Wednesday, April 8, 1936

"Come on, Molly. You're idling today." Edna nudged the mule's sides with her heels. It was a Possum Valley day, and she'd run late because, nearly a month later, Daddy's cough still lingered, and Edna had spent time making a mustard plaster for his chest. If she wanted to be honest, his cough concerned her. It appeared to have dug deeply into his lungs, and exhaustion shut his eyes constantly. She wished he could still talk so that she could ask him how he really felt. But the stroke had taken much of his speaking ability from him, as well as robbing him of the ability to walk and even to feed himself.

"Miss! Miss!" The child's voice jolted her out of her thoughts. She looked up to see the Holcomb boy who had been on patrol the last time she'd come. This time, though, he carried the picture book she'd left with the family. The rifle swung on its strap over his shoulder.

She pulled Molly to a halt. The mule snorted, as if to ask why they were stopping when she had just been told to hurry. "Yes?"

Running the short distance between them, the boy's breath came fast when he stopped. His overgrown hair flopping into his eyes as he squinted up at Edna. "Wantin' to swap books with ya, iffen that's alright. Ma asked if she can have somethin' this time, too – a mag'zine or what-have-ya. Somethin' with lots of pictures."

Edna Sue couldn't have kept the smile from blossoming on her face if she'd tried. "Certainly." She dug in her saddlebags and came up with two women's magazines – *The Woman's Home Companion* and *Modern Woman*. "Would your mother like me to come up to the house so she can choose between them?"

The boy shook his head. "Naw, not today. Ma's busy dousin' everybody's heads with vinegar. You'd be underfoot, see."

*Vinegar.* Edna Sue worked to keep the smile on her face. That meant that lice must be working their way through the family.

"Here ya go. That was a swell story, by the way. Can we have another one?" the boy asked as he shoved the picture book toward Edna.

Edna took it with hesitant fingers. She knew the lice couldn't travel with the books, but a shiver raced down her spine nonetheless. "Certainly. I'm glad you enjoyed it. And what's your name?" She pulled another picture book, *The Tale of Squirrel Nutkin*, from her saddlebag.

"Me? I'm Jim-Bob."

"Well, Jim-Bob, would you go to school if one opened near you?" She held her breath. This family had been the most open to the horseback library so far on this route; if they didn't cotton to the idea of a school, she didn't know if anyone would. *Why are you even asking? There's no teacher and no money to pay one! Mr. Gaunt confirmed that himself.*

The boy's eyes opened wide. "A school? A real school with books and... and paper and everything?"

"Yes. A real school."

He scratched his head, pulled something off his scalp, and peered at it before looking back up at Edna Sue. "Shucks, I dunno, miss. I dunno iffen we could afford that. But these books here – and Ma's magazine – we can pay for them in kind, ya know. We wouldn't want to be beholden, understand."

Saying that, he dug a hand into his pocket and pulled out a jar filled with something brown. "Ma said to give ya this – It's apple butter from last harvest – and to thank ya kindly for them books."

Edna Sue accepted the jar. "Thank you, Jim-Bob. And here are both the magazines; tell your mother that she can return them both to me next time."

He beamed and clutched the worn magazines and book to himself. "It's a pleasure, miss. Gotta get back to the house now. Ma'll be ready to vinegar me up."

The sun had begun its descent behind the western treeline when Edna Sue finally began riding toward her last stop of the route. A sense of pleasure filled her, very different from the discouragement she'd felt last time she'd ridden this route. Most of the folks at whose homes she'd stopped had taken something from her, whether a picture book, a Sunday School booklet, or a magazine. The only exception had been Mrs. McCabe, who had ordered Edna off her property once more. Even the blind Hansen couple had taken a picture book. Edna had discovered that Jim-Bob was their great-grandson and that he'd stopped by last time to share his own picture-book story with them, explaining in detail what the pictures looked to be telling about the story. Both old man and woman had given Edna Sue wide, toothless grins of delight when she'd told them she'd leave a book with them, too, for Jim-Bob to describe aloud when he came by.

Despite being nearly out of books, Edna's saddlebags still bulged – not with printed pages but with that jar of Vergie Holcomb's apple butter, a handful of nuts from the Field family, a bunch of the Schmidts' dried lavender, and a handed-down recipe for Indian cornbread, copied on a piece of faded newsprint by Wady O'Sullivan. *They'll never take something for nothing.* Edna Sue shook her head, a grudging admiration for the dignified pride of the mountain folk taking root in her.

A curl of smoke emerged from the trees ahead of her. Henry Ravenhill's place. *Why are you even bothering? He doesn't want any books.*

But Edna's curiosity was an itch she couldn't quite reach. *I should just leave him be. What business is it of mine why the man is here?*

Even as she thought it, though, she nudged Molly forward up the path, remaining on the lookout for that little black-and-white scamp of a dog.

Sure enough, as Molly's hooves clomped through the greening grass, the creature sprinted out of the bushes, a tornado of fluffy fur, loud yapping, and wagging tail. "Oh, you hush!" Edna called, not unkindly. "I think your bark is worse than your bite, that's for certain."

At Edna's voice, the little dog gave a few more woofs before running back through the bushes. When Edna emerged into the clearing minutes later, she saw the dog whining at the door of the cabin. She dismounted from Molly and tied the mule's reins to a low-hanging branch before approaching the porch cautiously. She'd always had a fondness for dogs, but she knew that it was better to be safe than sorry. Slowly she knelt beside the dog.

"Where's your master today? Huh?" As her hand lingered on the dog's silky fur, picking from it a dry leaf here, a little stick there, she let her gaze travel around the sloped clearing. It was already getting to midafternoon, and the trees threw the shadows down the hill toward her, making everything look a little more mysterious than usual. Her heart picked up its pace, and she breathed deeply to calm herself. Ben had told her that the one-armed man wasn't dangerous, regardless of how eccentric he might be. *I should probably just head back. It's getting late—*

The cabin creaked open. "Thought I told you I didn't want any of your books, miss."

She stumbled to her feet. She was relieved to see that he did not carry a rifle this time. Heartened by that observation, Edna Sue gathered her courage. "I did not take you seriously, sir."

His eyebrows rose, full and shaggy gray. At this proximity, Edna observed that he appeared deeply aged – like her father, well before his time. She also observed that amusement lurked in his expression.

"Mr. Ravenhill, isn't it? I'm Edna Sue O'Connell." She stuck out her hand.

A smile spread across the man's face. *Well, let him be amused!* Edna Sue kept her hand out.

At last, Ravenhill met her hand with his own weather-chapped one. "A pleasure to meet you, Miss O'Connell. I think I'd better ask you to come inside. Though, if I don't, I think you'll ask yourself in, won't you?"

Her mouth fell open, but she snapped it shut quickly.

"Come, Matilda," he beckoned the mutt, who scampered through the doorway. With that, Ravenhill entered his home, allowing Edna Sue to trail in his wake.

Cluttered. That was how Ravenhill's one-room cabin initially impressed Edna Sue. But then, as he eyes probed it, she found herself intrigued by the chaos surrounding her, hanging from the ceiling, choking the shelves that lined the walls, arranged in piles here-and-there-and-everywhere. An intricate Persian carpet blanketed the rough floor; a hand-carved bed – like her father's but, she had to admit, far more lovely – crouched in the corner; gleaming pans hung from hooks above the hot woodburning stove. And everywhere – everywhere – everywhere: books. Books of every shape and size, all well-used and stacked against one another.

"Oh, my." The words slipped out of her mouth as she gazed around the room.

He turned toward her with a knowing smile on his face. *No wonder he said he didn't need the books from Willow Hollow!* Embarrassment heated her, and she found distraction in removing her hat and coat and looking for a place to hang them.

"Over here," he gestured toward a couple of hooks fastened to the wall near the door. When she'd finished hanging them up, he moved toward the woodburning stove. "Will you be staying for supper, Miss O'Connell?"

"I...I couldn't..." She stumbled over her words, surprised by his sudden courtesy.

He lifted the lids on one of the pans that sat on the stove, and a cloud of fragrant steam rose. "I insist."

"It's a long ride back. I shouldn't have even stopped in today, but..."

He looked at her over his shoulder. "But what?"

She should just admit it. "But you piqued my curiosity last time, if you must know, Mr. Ravenhill."

A low chuckle came from the stove area. "Nosey female."

Offense ruffled Edna Sue's feathers, and she opened her mouth to protest, but he turned with a wink, disarming her when she realized he'd meant it humorously.

"I'm preparing lemon piccata. There is plenty for you, me, and even Matilda."

Lemon piccata? In the boondocks of Willow Hollow, Kentucky? The last time she'd had lemon piccata had been more than a decade ago, in New York. Her mouth watered as she recognized the bright, savory fragrance of the dish wafting through the cabin. "I suppose I could stay for just a bite or two."

Five minutes later, she and her host sat down to a white-clothed table. A steaming plate of pasta, crowned with a perfectly-browned chicken breast, swimming in a creamy lemon-and-caper sauce, adorned the place before each of them. Another, smaller plate sat beside Ravenhill's, bearing only a half-breast of chicken, cut into small pieces. Edna assumed it was for Matilda.

"This looks delicious." She picked up her fork and sank it into the breast before realizing that Ravenhill sat with his hand raised, his palm upward, and his eyes closed.

Ravenhill… was going to ask a blessing? Edna's fork froze in the chicken, and she allowed herself to simply stare at this odd man.

"For what we are about to receive, we are truly thankful unto Thee, O Lord. Amen."

He opened his eyes, catching her gaze with his, and smiled before picking up his knife with his one hand and, with precise and practiced movements, cutting his own chicken into pieces. They ate silently for several bites, Edna relishing the tangy creaminess of the sauce, the moist chicken, and the pasta she'd not enjoyed for far too long.

"It tastes wonderful," she finally said, breaking the silence. "May I ask, where you learned to cook this way? And how you came by such ingredients as capers and lemons in Willow Hollow?"

He flicked a bite to the dog, who swallowed it whole. "As for your first question, I have always enjoyed cooking and learned it from my mother. As to your second question, I have an old friend who visits me every few months. He came recently and brought the capers and lemons. I couldn't resist the opportunity to make this – one of my favorite dishes from… well, from long ago."

"I see." But she didn't really see at all. "Why…" She shook her head. It was none of her business, none at all.

"Why what?"

Well, he'd asked her to ask, hadn't he? She plunged forward. "Why are you here at all? You're an educated man – more educated than I am, clearly – well-read; cultured, though you try to hide it by waving that ridiculous gun around. You may not have—" And here she stopped, feeling an unaccustomed redness marching up her face.

He twirled his fork in his pile of pasta but lifted none to his mouth. "I may not have both my arms; isn't that what you were going to say, Miss O'Connell?"

She might as well admit it. "Yes," she said boldly. "It just seems like you are wasting your life, Mr. Ravenhill. Some of us are stuck here in the mountains, but you seem to have chosen to be here."

He remained quiet for a long moment. Then he put down his fork, still looking into his half-eaten meal. "I have chosen it – for a time."

"But why?" Her own meal forgotten, Edna Sue stared at him, exposing her full curiosity.

His good hand came up to touch the place where his other arm should have linked to his shoulder but did not. "I needed time apart, away from the world. Even away from other believers."

Something hardened in Edna Sue when she heard that word. She sat back in her chair and folded her arms across her chest. "Believers? Are you one of those born-again people?" *Like Daddy. Like Mother.* Both had come to Christ, as they put it, during a tent revival meeting in New York; that was where, too, Daddy had sensed his "calling" to return as a medical missionary to the Appalachians.

A faint smile touched Ravenhill's lips. "Yes, yes, you could say that. You see, Miss O'Connell, many years ago, when I was around the age I would assume you are, I was a theologian rising in the ranks of my colleagues. Pressed to become someone, to do something for God. I had talent – oh, did I have talent. I was gifted in language study beyond many of my peers. I had come from a prestigious religious family, and I had married a woman who embodied the lauded Biblical virtues of womanhood. We had a beautiful boy named Theodore – Teddy

– after my father. I was careful to do right, to repent of my small sins (as I thought of them), to help the poor, to lead my family aright. Everything was correct. At least, outwardly."

"Outwardly?"

He nodded. "Yes. Though I knew that all I had was only by God's grace, I also sensed that I had given Him no reason to withhold His blessing from my life."

Edna couldn't help herself from leaning forward. "And what happened?"

He looked across the room, as if visualizing the events of which he spoke. "Looking back, I see that it began on the day, at the incredibly young age of thirty-five, I was offered the position of president of the Trinity School of Theology. I left the board meeting with a song of praise in my heart to the Lord.

"Yet, when I arrived home, eager to tell Tabitha, my wife, the news, I found a policeman at our door." He swallowed and shook his head. "My little son had been involved in an automobile accident with a family friend. A horse had spooked at the noisy engine, and…" He clamped his jaw for a long moment before going on. "I rushed to the hospital, where Tabitha waited, nearly mad with grief. Our Teddy… Well, the doctors had been unable to save him. In a moment, my life had turned upside down."

Silence prevailed for a moment. Edna Sue felt as though she could hear her own heartbeat. Did she really want to hear this story about which she had been so curious? The pain of it made her want to turn away. "Please, you don't have to…"

But Ravenhill appeared determined to finish what he'd begun. "On the day after Teddy's funeral, we received further shocking news. My father, whose business interests had always gone so smoothly, had lost the vast majority of his wealth – of our family's wealth, for I was heavily invested in his textile mill – in a bad deal. There was barely enough income for us to continue living in the somewhat-lavish style to which we'd grown accustomed, unless I entered into the presidency of the

Trinity School. Numb from grief over Teddy's death, nearly unable to think, this was, of course, the last thing I wanted to do, but I accepted the position out of necessity."

Edna blinked against the agony she heard still ringing in his voice.

"The day before my installation, however, a young woman approached Trinity's board. She hailed from the first church I had pastored. She claimed... She claimed that she and I were engaged in an inappropriate relationship." He looked straight at Edna, his jaw tight. "An adulterous relationship."

"Was it true?" The question popped out of Edna's mouth. "I'm sorry... I..."

But Ravenhill shook his head. "No, it was not true. I still cannot understand why she would seek to harm my family that way. She retracted her story later. But the damage had already been done. The Trinity board apologetically asked me to resign out of concern for the school's reputation. Broken, I acquiesced, thinking that my wife and I would seek a small church to pastor, where we could try to recover from the emotional trauma we'd endured. Where I could seek to understand this God I had long worshipped but must have never truly known. But it was not to be."

"What happened?" Edna knew something had. She saw it on his face.

He clenched his jaw, not in anger but in grief. "Tabitha... She had already had a difficult time dealing with our son's death, the financial struggles, the accusations and the loss of our reputations. I tried to bury myself in my studies, in my work, but the empty house was to her a constant reminder of what God had taken from us. And then... the final blow came."

Matilda whined near the door, and Ravenhill rose to let the dog outside. Edna Sue saw that dusk quickly descended, but she couldn't leave in the middle of this story; she simply couldn't.

The chair creaked as Ravenhill took his seat once more.

"It will sound unbelievable to you after everything else that occurred, but I am going to tell it as it happened. We moved into the parsonage that came as part of our salary with the desperate church that hired me. I needed to get all of our furniture into the house, but no one was available to help me with it. So I did it alone. Or tried to, at least. Getting the antique bureau upstairs proved too much for me. Halfway up the narrow staircase, I slipped and fell all the way down. The bureau fell, too – right on top of my arm."

Edna's mouth fell open for not the first time that day. "But surely, it was only a break. Surely, that isn't why your arm…"

He shook his head. "They couldn't save it. I woke in the hospital, with one arm."

Edna Sue stared. "That's terrible."

"It was." He stood, taking Edna's plate as well as his own over to the wash basin. "But what was worse happened the next day."

*Worse? How could this story get worse?*

"When Tabitha came to the hospital to see me, I saw that she had become a shell of the woman of faith I knew. When, in my agony, I asked her if she would pray with me, she broke into laughter and said… She told me that, if I had any brains left, I should curse God and die."

*Curse God and die.* Had not the same thought run through Edna's own mind during these years of looking after Daddy? "I feel like I understand her, though."

Ravenhill returned to the table and sat down. "Oh?"

Edna sat up straight and shrugged. "You had served God so well. Is that the kind of payment you should expect? That she should have expected?" The defiance energized her, made her raise her chin as she looked Ravenhill straight in the eyes.

"Payment?" Ravenhill repeated. "Serving God is not a business arrangement. That, perhaps, is part of what I had to learn, Miss O'Connell. He owes me nothing. But He gives us His love."

"I'll bet your wife doesn't think much of God's love." She knew her words held a barb, but she couldn't help it.

He stayed quiet, jaw pulsing. She wondered for a moment if he was angry, but when he lifted his eyes to meet hers again, she saw that he had been trying to restrain the tears that had arisen. "She... Tabitha took her own life."

Uneasily, Edna shifted on her chair, thinking of the evening when she'd thought of throwing herself over the edge of Scarlet Ridge. "And you? What did you do?" she asked, hearing the uncustomary softness in her own voice.

"I came here. I couldn't bear to be around people for some time. I felt that I needed to come apart, to learn of God again, to seek to understand Him, to ask Him the questions that shredded my heart. My dear friend – the same one who still brings me food supplies now and then – had built a retreat cabin up here on a piece of property that had been in his family for generations. He told me I was welcome to stay as long as I liked. I've been here now for nearly fifteen years."

A quietness stretched between them before she voiced the question rushing to her lips, "And did He ever answer you?"

Ravenhill cocked his head.

"You said that there were questions that had shredded your heart." Did not the same sensation affect her? "Did God ever answer you?"

Ravenhill looked at the remnants of his supper. "I found that, when I sought answers, I really needed God Himself, not the answers. When I came face-to-face with Him, He Himself was all the answer I needed this side of eternity, Miss O'Connell. That was a long time coming to me, but, in the end, I found what I really sought. Don't we all?"

He really needed God Himself... Edna swallowed down the rebellion that rose in her throat. *Curse God and die.* Or bless Him and live? Could there be truth in that? She shook away the troubling thoughts.

Matilda scratched at the door, and Ravenhill rose, let the

dog in, and sat back down again. The little mutt curled up with her head on his feet.

"Will you ever return to the world?" Edna ventured to ask.

Ravenhill looked down for a moment before answering. "I've been thinking recently that perhaps I am ready to return to the land of the living. But I've felt hesitant to leave the seclusion I've come to love so much." He grimaced a smile at Edna Sue. "That reluctance to give up my solitude led to my rudeness the first day I met you. I'm sorry that I tried to scare you off with my rifle. It isn't—"

"It isn't loaded; I know." Edna let a little smile turn up the corner of her lips. "My cousin Ben Thrasher told me. But I think the mountain ways must be rubbing off on you, Mr. Ravenhill. Would you ever have waved a rifle – loaded or unloaded – at a woman back at the School of Theology?"

Ravenhill winced sheepishly.

"I think it is time you returned to the land of the living, for your own sanity," she went on.

"Perhaps." He smiled faintly. "And what of you, Miss O'Connell? What is a well-educated, well-spoken young woman doing in the mountains of Kentucky? Did you come to be a horseback librarian?"

Her mouth twisted. *Young woman.* That she certainly no longer was. "No. Certainly not." She traced the edge of the white tablecloth with her finger. For some reason, this little cabin, so removed from all she knew, felt like a safe place to speak all she'd never said. "My father moved us here when I was a young child. He hailed from the mountains as a boy, left them to become a doctor, and then returned with my mother and me." Her jaw tightened. "My mother didn't last long here. She was born with a delicate constitution, besides coming from a very different life. Once upon a time, she'd been told that she had a future as a great pianist." Sometimes Edna Sue felt like she could still hear her mother playing lullabies as Edna Sue took her afternoon nap on the chaise-lounge in Grandmother's parlor.

She looked up to see Ravenhill's eyes steadily on her. He waited for her to continue. So she did. "My mother died less than a year after we moved here. Grandmother begged Daddy to allow her to raise me in the city after that, if Daddy refused all common-sense and wouldn't leave these godforsaken mountains himself. But Daddy did refuse on both accounts. And then he remarried a local woman he'd known as a boy. My stepmother made it clear to me whenever Daddy was away – which was often, since he spent more and more time tending to the sick after Mother's death – that she saw me as a source of trouble and work."

Her voice quieted as the layers of pain peeled back. It felt as though a scab had been loosened off a pus-filled wound – painful yet relieving all at once.

"I grew to hate these mountains. Daddy continued to say that God had a purpose for the pain we saw on a daily basis; that part of the reason we were here was to help alleviate the suffering around us, not to merely gain pleasure for ourselves. But I felt as though my whole life had been one long experience of suffering – both on my own behalf and on the behalf of others. Sometimes, I would go out and sit by Mother's grave – and wish that I, too, had died and gone from this world of woe, this world which God tormented.

"At last, I got my chance at escape. When I was a teenager, my stepmother got into an argument with me in front of my father – such a severe one that I really believe that his eyes at last opened to her dislike of me. Determined to stay in the mountains himself, Daddy wrote to my grandmother in the city and asked that I be permitted to live with her and gain a real education. My grandmother, thrilled at the proposal, welcomed me into her life and home. And so I lived in New York for several years, graduating from high school and finishing my teaching degree. That, Mr. Ravenhill, is how I gained my education."

He smiled. "I see. And how is it that you landed back here in Kentucky, then?"

She clenched her jaw again. "I received a letter – over ten years ago now – from Ruthie, my stepmother, telling me that Daddy had suffered a massive stroke and was at death's door." How well she remembered the tension of love and anger that had rendered her heart as she'd read Ruthie's dictated letter. "Even my grandmother insisted that I should travel back here. At the time, I thought it was only to say goodbye." She dropped her eyes. How could she admit this? But the words slipped out. "I welcomed the journey, in all honesty. I was glad to put Daddy and these mountains and their tormenting God behind me at last and for good – to have all that attached me to these mountains buried forever beneath the soil."

"But you're still here." Ravenhill cocked his head in question.

The familiar depression shadowed her heart. "Yes. When I arrived, Daddy's condition had stabilized. He had lost all capacity to speak, to feed himself, and to walk, but he appeared to have drawn back from death's door. My stepmother, however, in the years since I left the mountains, had steadily declined in health – or at least, that's what she says. We argued terribly. She insisted on staying with Daddy at Scarlet Ridge Farm – and insisted, too, that she needed me to support and assist her. I wanted to bring Daddy back to the city, where the medical profession had advanced and new therapies might help him regain some of his mobility – where I could hire a professional nurse with my teaching income and the profits from the farm's sale. My grandmother even offered her financial support for their removal from the mountains to the city. But you can see who won that argument."

In the silence, the wood crackled in the stove. Edna Sue allowed her eyes to drift around the cabin. Her glance landed on a small plaque. Carved into the wood, she read:

*"Though He slay me, yet will I trust in Him."*

What a joke. "You still believe there is a good God, after all the evil that has happened to you, Mr. Ravenhill?" *Happened to you in His Name, doing His work,* she might add, but didn't.

His lashes closed softly over his eyes. "I do. Even so. How could I believe that evil exists if I didn't believe in its opposite?"

She shook her head roughly against that notion. "If there is a God—" The sudden lump in her throat threatened to choke her and she swallowed it down. "If there is a God, I have a bone to pick with Him. He has ruined my life over and over again, from when I was a child until now. He has crushed all of my dreams, destroyed any chance of a real future." *And killed my love for Daddy.* "If I could stand before Him and present my case, I'm certain I would win the argument." And how satisfying that would be!

He raised an eyebrow. "For someone who claims to disbelieve in God, you seem fairly certain that He exists."

Ouch. She'd never thought of that. "I—"

He raised a hand. "Have you ever asked God, Miss O'Connell?"

"Asked Him what?"

"Your questions."

She gave a humorless laugh. "Yes. Long ago, and there was silence."

Ravenhill sat silently for a long moment, staring down into his coffee mug. *Nothing to say now? No platitude?*

She rose from the table. "Well, thank you for the meal. It was truly the best I've eaten in ten years, I think."

He stood as well, following her to the door, still quiet.

But as her feet stepped out the door, Ravenhill broke his silence. "God isn't ours, Miss O'Connell, in the way that Matilda is 'my' dog. We can't force Him to answer us; He doesn't owe us that. Though He also doesn't turn away our honest questions."

When she turned, Edna saw that a smile niggled the corner of the man's lips. "Though I think, when we do seek answers, we will find more than we bargained for. We may find Him, Himself – as I did."

His eyes told of no defeat at her hands. Rather a quiet confidence – and was it pity as well? – filled them. "We all have our own secret place of thunder, Miss O'Connell." He stepped back inside the house. "Goodbye for now. Come again when you can."

*"We all have our own secret place of thunder."* As Molly picked her careful way down the mountain path, Edna Sue puzzled over Ravenhill's words. What could they mean?

Darkness already cloaked Scarlet Ridge as Edna Sue rode into the farmyard. A mountain cat yowled in the distance, and she couldn't prevent the shudder that the sound sent down her spine. In recent years, she'd often prided herself on her independent streak, on her fearlessness, on her freedom from mountain superstition – including their belief in this omnipotent God – the God who had killed her mother, who'd struck Daddy, who'd saddled Edna Sue with a partially-bedridden stepmother, who'd taken away her job. If she had believed in Him, that is.

But her conversation with Ravenhill over a cityfied meal had dealt an unexpected blow to the self-assurance she'd cultivated for years, had caused questions to rise, ghostly bodies from the deep graves she'd long-ago dug for them.

And the haunting brought little comfort. With firmness, she pushed aside the disturbing thoughts and started her evening chores. She had no time for such nonsense as Ravenhill spouted. Ruthie surely would complain already about Edna's overdue arrival.

# 9

## Saturday, May 2, 1936

"Miss O'Connell!"

*Cecil Gaunt.* The warm voice beckoned Edna to turn her head. She'd not spoken with him in more than two weeks, and then it had only been to quickly exchange new books for the ones the schoolchildren had finished reading. Now, torn between giving in to or ignoring the teacher's friendliness, she hesitated with one foot inside the Building's entrance.

"Miss O'Connell," he called again, nearer this time.

Decisively, she turned. "Yes, Mr. Gaunt?"

He limped his way across the dusty street. "Glad I caught you." His sincere – well, it looked that way, at least – smile threatened to disarm her.

"Oh? Why is that?" She kept her voice cool, sharply contrasting with the warm spring day.

"I have these books to return to you."

For the first time, she noticed the short stack tucked in the crook of Cecil's arm.

"I hope you don't mind, but I kept out *Treasure Island*. We finished the term yesterday, but I personally would like to read that one myself. I never got to it as a boy." He offered her the stack.

She couldn't stop the smile that pulled at her own lips as

she took the stack from him. "I'm glad they enjoyed the books. But you could have simply brought them back to the library. You don't need to return them to me, you know."

The smile grew. "I wanted to give them back to you, Miss O'Connell. It gave me the opportunity to speak with you."

His words goaded Edna's heart into double-time. *Stop that. You're being ridiculous.* Cecil Gaunt was a hick-country schoolteacher with half-a-brain if he stayed in Willow Hollow by choice. Someone like Ivory or Lillian or Lena was much more up his alley, if he had romantic intentions.

"I wanted to tell you how much the students enjoyed them."

Even as her heart drooped, Edna knew a little painful satisfaction. See, nothing beyond courtesy had motivated his words.

"Do you have time to come to my house for the noon dinner?"

She tensed. "Why?" she asked bluntly.

He shaded his eyes against the brightness of the sun. "Because I have an idea for you."

"For me?" She frowned, wishing he would just spit out whatever he meant. "What is it?"

He shook his head. "If I tell you here, you won't come to my house for dinner. And it's a pity to eat dinner alone if you can eat it with a friend."

She almost snickered at that. "Friends? Is that what you think we are, Mr. Gaunt?"

He looked surprised. "I hope so, Miss O'Connell. Wouldn't you say so?"

All because she'd spoken to him a couple of times about books! She bit her lip. "All right, I will come if that's what it takes to hear your idea."

He winked. "I hope this means you agree."

"About what?"

"That we're friends."

His persistence silenced her protest, and she shook her head in exasperation. "I can't stay long. I need to get back to the farm early this afternoon."

"I won't keep you longer than the time it takes to eat and explain my idea," he promised. "Shall we?"

---

Ten minutes later, Cecil placed a steaming bowl of thick soup before his guest. "It's not fancy, but it'll fill you up." He gripped the back of his own chair tightly as he lowered himself into his seat. Thank the Lord above that he'd not taken another tumble yet, as he'd done upon the occasion of his first meeting with Miss Edna Sue O'Connell!

Miss O'Connell appeared to let the distinct aroma of the meal meet her nostrils. "Burgoo?"

Cecil nodded and wondered if he should have simply served jam sandwiches. The mountain concoction of chicken meat and livers, plus beans and vegetables, probably didn't meet with the librarian's sophisticated tastes.

But Miss O'Connell moved her hand to pick up the spoon beside her bowl.

"Shall I ask the blessing?" He asked it as a question, but he didn't dare wait for her answer before he bowed his head. "We thank Thee, Lord, for this good food Thou hast placed upon our table. We thank Thee for the minds Thou has given us. May we use them for Thy glory. In the Name of Thy Son, amen."

Opening his eyes, he added his own silent plea for the Almighty's guidance and plunged forward. "Now, I won't beat around the bush." He dipped his spoon into the chunky broth, though his stomach rolled. "I've been giving your idea of a school up in Possum Valley more thought, especially now that our own school year is behind us."

Intense interest glimmered in Miss O'Connell's eyes

before she dropped her gaze back to her soup. "Oh?" Her tone pretended nonchalance.

"And I wonder – what if you taught the school yourself, Miss O'Connell? Starting in the fall term? You've mentioned to me that you obtained your teaching degree."

"I haven't the time."

She didn't even hesitate; Cecil's gut sank further, but he pressed on. "Not even for a once-a-week school? Just to give the children some education – to teach them their letters and numbers? I know that you ride your library routes twice-a-week, sometimes thrice, but perhaps on Fridays or Mondays? And I have been thinking about the highlanders' inability to pay; what if they paid you in jam and eggs – things like that?"

Miss O'Connell shook her head vigorously. "I've told you; I haven't the time. Besides…" Her words trailed off, and she stirred her soup, her hand tense on the spoon.

So the time wasn't the real issue. Cecil leaned forward. "Besides…?"

She met his gaze, eyes daring him to contradict her. "Besides, I won't be here forever."

Something clenched in Cecil's chest at her claim. "Oh?" he managed. "I thought you had family here."

She shook her head. "Only my father – and a few cousins here-and-there – and when my father passes…" Again, she trailed off, and Cecil noted the pang that seized her expression for a moment, though she drove it away nearly as quickly as it had appeared.

"I see." *Concentrate on the burgoo, Cecil.* He lifted a spoonful to his mouth and chewed.

Across from him, Miss O'Connell shifted uneasily. Her tone altered, too, from – well, if not warmth, at least neutrality into coldness. "You'd be a fool to stay forever yourself, Mr. Gaunt. Perhaps you'll come to your senses one of these days. Perhaps when you lose – What did you call it once? Hope?" She snorted a laugh. "Yes, just wait until you, too, lose hope. Then

I wager you'll pack your bags quickly enough and shake the dust of these mountains from your feet forever."

Pity rushed into the creekbed of his heart. He swallowed and laid his spoon down beside his bowl. "I already lost hope once, Miss O'Connell when I thought that it found its source in the things of this world – and in myself." He smiled, praying for the truth to come as gently as she needed it. "As I've told you before, I know now that true hope comes from outside myself – and from outside this world. It comes from the One who made the world."

She sniffed her disdain aloud, and he shed inward tears. "You seek fulfillment and hope in the wrong places, Miss O'Connell." He paused. "I hope you don't find me too bold in saying so."

Across from him, she bristled like a porcupine but answered calmly. "Not at all, Mr. Gaunt."

"It saddens me because I see such potential in you." The words bubbled out.

A laugh met them. "Potential? These mountains have sucked dry my potential, Mr. Gaunt, so I'm not sure of what you speak. In the city, I could have made something of myself; I could have accomplished much, but here... here, all is wasted."

"Perhaps, it's a matter of perspective. Some think of potential in terms of personal achievement. I think of potential in terms of what you can do for others to honor the Name of Christ. Perhaps if you sought that kind of fulfillment, Miss O'Connell, well, then you might find that your scope is limitless, even in Willow Hollow."

She stared at him, and, even though he knew that he spoke the truth, Cecil felt himself redden under her contempt. "Isn't that what I'm doing already? I'm fulfilling my duties to my father and to my stepmother, if that's what you mean."

For a split second, he wished that he could let it go, but he cared about her too much to do that. "But do you fulfill them from the heart? Or merely from, well, self-righteousness?"

Her spoon clanged down to the table. "Self-righteousness belongs to the religious, Mr. Gaunt. I forsook my father's God when He forsook me – long ago."

One corner of Cecil's mouth turned up. "Self-righteousness belongs to the religious? Or is it just a way for all of us to justify ourselves to our own consciences?" he asked, his voice soft.

Miss O'Connell rose with an abruptness that banged the legs of her chair against the wooden floor. "I think I've had quite enough preaching for the day. Thank you for dinner." She folded her napkin neatly and placed it beside her plate. "I'll see myself out."

"Miss O'Connell, I—" He struggled to stand up, but his guest closed the front door behind her before he could.

Heart heavy in his chest, Cecil stacked the bowls and spoons in his washbasin and headed outside. Some of his best praying was done in company with the tomatoes.

---

Her feet etched themselves in Main Street's dirt as Edna marched her way to the General Store. Ignorant man! Spouter of religious platitudes! Cecil Gaunt had no notion of what he was talking about.

But if so… why then did Edna's jaw clamp hard against the scalding tears that rose to conquer her? *He doesn't know me. He has no right, no right at all to question my motives!* She climbed up the two steps to the store with more strength than required and pushed open the door. Its windows were some of the only ones in town made of glass, rather than waxed paper.

The bell above the door jingled her arrival, and Pearl Clark, proprietress, snapped up her thin neck to peer at Edna. "Oh, it's you, Edna Sue." She sounded as though she'd rather see a fox making off with one of her laying hens than greet Edna.

*Good afternoon to you, too, Pearl.* She and Pearl had attended Willow Hollow's one-room school together many years ago, and Edna hadn't cottoned to her then – nor Pearl to Edna. But Edna knew that she should be glad for the trading business she and the Clarks conducted; it helped to supplement her librarian income, for sure.

"I brought you some more cheese and soap if you can use it." Edna opened the satchel she carried and withdrew some of the wrapped goods.

Pearl pursed her lips. "Well, now, I don't reckon we done run outta what ya brung last time…"

Edna locked Pearl with a stare. *She wants me to beg.* She lifted her chin. "Oh, really? Mr. Armstrong told me you were out of soap. Actually, he asked me if he could just buy from me directly. Perhaps I'd better do—"

"Now, hold on, hold on. Don't be hasty. I only said that I didn't reckon. What, do you expect me to keep track of every little thing in this store – besides my work with the post office?"

"I'm sure that – what? – three letters incoming a week are taxing to body and mind, Pearl." All of the sarcasm she'd wished she'd spewed on Mr. Gaunt now dripped off Edna's words. The Clarks' store hosted the town's post office, but rarely did more than a few pieces of mail pass over the counter weekly.

Pearl sniffed and whipped away, turning her back to Edna. "I'm busy right now. Leave your soap and cheese on the counter, and I'll credit it to your account."

A small smile of victory tipped Edna's lips. She placed the small packages on the counter. "I'll take some of Widow Crawley's honey while I'm here."

Pearl snapped shut the ledger book and sighed. But she still moved toward the shelf behind the counter on which she displayed jars of the deep golden honey. "Large or small?"

"Small."

Pearl set the jar before Edna with a forcefulness just shy

of cracking it. "Anything else?"

"No."

"Using your store credit?"

Edna bit the inside of her lip as she calculated what they'd have left on their account if she did. "Yes."

"Fine."

She picked up the jar, not expecting a *have-a-good-day*, and turned to leave.

But Pearl's voice stopped her before she managed to get a foot out the door. "Almost slipped my mind. Got a letter for ya."

A letter? The words stopped Edna in her tracks. She couldn't keep away the surprise that was writing itself across her face as she turned back to face Pearl.

Pearl held out the envelope. "Came real late. Got delayed some 'cause of that bridge wash-out, I reckon. Hope it's nothin' requirin' immediate attention."

Retracing her steps, Edna took the envelope, the sealing's stickiness coming off on her fingers. She raised her eyebrows at Pearl, but the woman only blinked at her, innocent as… *as a raccoon washing his stolen supper.* More than once, Edna had suspected a letter might have been steamed open and then resealed. Pearl surely intended no harm by it – Edna knew that idle curiosity spurred on the woman – but having someone snooping into her private affairs irked her nonetheless.

Edna gave a curt nod of thanks and exited the store, trying to control her excitement: The letter bore her grandmother's penmanship. As she made her way back to the hitching post in front of the store, Edna Sue felt every crinkle and corner of the envelope in her pocket.

A letter for her.

From New York City.

The first in ten years.

And it had been delayed for weeks!

She tugged Molly's reins free of the post, looped them back around the mule's neck, and hesitated. The letter nearly had a pulse, or was that her own blood pounding in anticipation? She clenched her teeth. *Wait. You must wait until you get out of town.* If she didn't, she knew that everyone would be talking of how she'd gotten a letter. And no wonder, when Willow Hollow only had a few pieces of mail come through a month – and rarely any for the O'Connells.

She managed only a few paces before she couldn't stand the suspense any longer. Reining Molly to a halt, Edna Sue swung off and led the animal to the hitching post in front of the Building. Her fingers shook as she drew the letter out of her pocket. Hopefully, here, the few folks passing by would think that she read library material of some sort or another.

The fine paper envelope sported the unmistakable cursive of Mrs. Althea Cummings – Edna's grandmother, her mother's mother. Her breath bated, Edna traced a shaking finger over the elegant loops and curls. Grandmother had not written a single word to her for over a decade – ever since Edna Sue had decided to stay in Willow Hollow and take care of Daddy, rather than to leave him in the care of Ruthie and Fate. Grandmother had not understood that Ruthie could not – or would not – care for Daddy alone. *Daddy would have died if I'd left.*

And perhaps that end would have set fine with Grandmother, too.

Edna Sue shook her head with violence. No, that couldn't be. Even if Grandmother openly despised Daddy for taking away her only daughter, Edna's mother, she could not have wished him dead, surely… She simply had not understood the true situation.

Which had made her rejection of Edna Sue even harder to bear.

A decade-old rejection that now rose up in the form of this letter to confront Edna. *What can she possibly have to say?*

Her fingers numb, she struggled to break the seal and then pulled two crisp sheets from their paper jacket.

*April 2, 1936*

*My dear granddaughter,*

*You may well wonder that I call you, "dear," having dismissed contact with you for the past several years. I was angry with you – no, more to the point, angry with your father, for once more taking away my only grandchild, depriving both you and me of the beautiful life together I had envisioned for us. Angry, too, that he would not listen to reason even in his illness and insisted on staying in the mountains that had robbed him of not only his precious wife – my daughter – but also now had taken his health. As you well know, had he returned to the city, I would have financially provided for his medical care and habitation, but once more he allowed pride to rule him.*

*But all of that is in the past, or could be. For the years have cooled my anger, and gray now covers my head with greater speed than it once did. I will be eighty years old at my next birthday, Edna, and I wish for you to celebrate it with me at my home in New York City. I have something important that I wish you to consider, and I want to speak about it with you in person. Perhaps we can put the years of separation behind us and make a new start together.*

*But I am getting ahead of myself. Enclosed, you will find a blank check which I have signed and addressed to you. Use it to purchase whatever you need to travel to me.*

*As I hope that you recall, my birthday falls on the twelfth of May, so this will provide you with plenty of time to plan.*

*Affectionately,*
*Althea Cummings*

The letter stunned Edna as much as a two-by-four to her forehead would have. No apology found its way into the missive – she had never expected that – but she knew that this invitation stood as an olive branch.

*"We could make a new start together."*

But how could she do that when her duty remained with Daddy here, much as the thought turned her stomach into a clod of frozen mud? Just as a decade ago, she couldn't abandon him now. A lump rose in her throat. He was still her father, despite everything he had done, all his "pride" as Grandmother called it, that had forced the family into the mountains so that he could play doctor-savior to these stiff-necked country bumpkins who had never appreciated him!

*If only Daddy would let me take him back to the city!*

But she knew he never would. He would let her go, but he himself had cemented his feet to the soil of these Kentucky hills. Even in his nearly-speechless state, he had made that much clear.

A horse whinnied in the street nearby, startling Edna. She tucked the letter back into her pocket and mounted Molly. As she rode out of town, she kept her expression void as usual, but her mind somersaulted.

She had to go to New York City for Grandmother's birthday. She had to. She could get someone – maybe even her cousin Ben – to help out at Scarlet Ridge Farm. She'd pay him, of course, though Ben would resist being compensated for helping out a family member. Surely, too, Curt would give her the time off.

Yes, she would go.

---

Ruthie's crossed arms and glare would have sent an ornery goat running for the hills, but Edna refused to buckle. "Just where did you take off to today?" her stepmother demanded as Edna neared the threshold.

"To town."

"And why, I'd like to know? It's not a library day, of that much I'm certain. And I know you ain't got yourself a beau."

Ruthie harrumphed a cheerless laugh. "A man might as well take up with a serpent as with you."

Edna forced her hurt feelings to lie still below the surface of her heart. Wordlessly, she pushed past Ruthie and entered the cabin's gloom.

"Your daddy's took sicker again. Not that you'd care a whit."

Ruthie's voice scraped Edna's ears. Her eyes darted toward Daddy's chair – now empty. A cough rasped from the darkness of the bed. Edna froze for a moment, then she dropped the saddlebags she carried right there on the floor and hurried to his side.

She strained to see in the darkness. "Why didn't you light the lamps?" she demanded without looking back at Ruthie.

"Said the light bothered him. 'Sides, we have precious little oil left." Edna Sue heard Ruthie shuffle up behind her. Her eyes had adjusted, and she gritted her teeth at the sight of Daddy's gray face and closed eyes.

"You should've told me. I could have bought some while I was in town. I could've taken more eggs or milk to the Clarks. They'd have put it up against our account." She placed a hand to Daddy's forehead but jerked it away at the heat radiating from his skin.

"Mebbe ya should get Doc Casey to take a look at him."

Edna sniffed. "I wouldn't trust that backwoods doctor with a cat I liked." Even to her, her words sounded unfair. So the doctor hadn't been educated as finely as Daddy; he still knew medicine. Yet she didn't want to take back her words in the face of Ruthie's snarl. She rose to her feet. Nothing could be accomplished for Daddy's benefit by her kneeling by his side. "Didn't you think to make a mustard plaster for his chest?" she flung out as she made her way toward the kitchen area.

Ruthie stayed silent, her arms crossed, her shoulders bowed over. As Edna stirred together the ingredients for the plaster, though, the older woman spoke up again, this time in a more subdued tone. "Iffen you'd butcher a chicken, I'll make him a broth."

Edna Sue added another chunk of wood to the stove to increase its heat before turning to Ruthie. "Alright. I'll be back. Finish the plaster, will you?"

As she opened the door to step into the night, Ruthie's murmured jab reached her ears, "This wouldn't have happened if you'd just kept to the farm."

# 10

Over the weekend, the letter from Grandmother sat heavily in Edna Sue's pocket, but Edna didn't feel right opening and considering it again while Daddy grew worse before her eyes. *Isn't this what I longed for, deep in my heart?* She shook away the thought. *No, no, of course not.* Yet why did she feel guilt and fear at this turn of events?

If only there was someone in whom she could confide! Confide? Since when had she felt that need?

*Always.* Her awareness of her accustomed loneliness had grown as Daddy worsened, drawing ever further from her physically. She had realized how far emotionally she had kept everyone in her effort to be independent and in control... and how it had drained her of love, both given and received. Yet how could she ever change now? She felt helpless in the face of her own responses.

On Monday, she made certain that Daddy would be as comfortable as possible and then told Ruthie that she needed to ride up the mountain.

"What fer?" Ruthie squinted at her as she heated Daddy's broth – not that he sipped much of it. "Ain't a book day."

Impatience rose in her. Why should Ruthie think that Edna needed to answer to her? "I have someone with whom I need to speak. I'll be back before supper." She turned and snatched her hat off its nail by the door.

"Someone you gotta speak to? Who'd you know up there?" Ruthie called after her. "Sure hope 'tain't that Ravenhill fellow! I tol' ya to stay away from him! 'Sides, there's a storm a-coming."

Ravenhill was exactly who Edna planned to see. Something about the man drew her, though she knew that everything about his situation and himself should repel her. She tacked up Molly, glancing at the gray sky lowering overhead. *I'll get back early, as I told Ruthie.* No spring storm could be worse, surely, than the one that had washed out the bridge back in March.

---

Thunder rumbled, and Cecil lifted his head from his book at the sound. A smile rose to his lips. How he loved late spring rains – softening the earth, making it ready for all things to grow again. He bit back a wince as he pushed himself to his feet. Seeing the first raindrops hit the ground would be worth the effort.

Throwing open the front door of his cottage, he stood at the threshold and watched the storm clouds ripple, heavy and ripe with rain, across the sky. *The heavens declare the glory of God; and the firmament sheweth His handiwork.*

It would be beautiful to watch this storm from a high vantage point. Perhaps up near Scarlet Ridge Farm...

He smiled at his own foolishness. First of all, he didn't even know exactly where Scarlet Ridge Farm was located. Second, after the tenseness of their last meeting, would Edna Sue show him any welcome if he came uninvited onto her property? Surely, she wouldn't pull out a rifle, as the parents of some of his students had done a time or two, but she could sure send a bullet from that mouth of hers when she wanted to.

That mouth of hers – quick to purse in frustration, quick to unleash her intelligence in words; slow to smile and speak in kindness, but when it did… it was lovely as that red, red rose of which the poet Burns spoke. He imagined it would be very nice to watch a storm come with her by his side.

Ten minutes later, Cecil found himself striding into Pastor Stuart's livery stable. "Good afternoon, Jed," he greeted the reverend's teenaged son.

"Hiya, Mr. Gaunt," Jed answered from where he sat on a bale of hay, saddle-soaping a bridle. "What brings you here?"

Cecil reached down to give a pat to Mittens the cat, who snaked through his legs. "I'm looking to rent a horse for a few hours."

Jed's eyebrows rose. "In this weather? You'll get awful wet, Mr. Gaunt. Sure it can't wait?"

Cecil shook his head. "I'm sure. I want to see this beautiful storm from a higher vantage point – I was thinking of Scarlet Ridge Farm. If you will give me directions, that is."

Jed shrugged. "Okay. That's Doc O'Connell's land, but he won't care iffen you want to enjoy it. And you can ride Ginger. Her name's fiery, but she's as tame as one of Mitten's kittens."

---

Thunder growled above her head and rain began to fall harder as Edna Sue made the last turn onto Ravenhill's property. She wondered why Matilda hadn't come out to greet her, as the mutt usually did. *Must be hiding out from the damp.* Most dogs she'd known in her life had only tolerated, not enjoyed, wet weather.

She led Molly into the shelter of the shed and tied her there, grateful for the respite from the rain the shelter provided. Leaving the mule with a nose-sack of grain to keep occupied for a while, Edna Sue jogged toward the house, dodging the growing puddles and holding her hat fast to her head.

It was only when she stood in front of the tightly-closed

door that she began to doubt her coming at all. Why *had* she come?

*I'm looking for answers.* The realization rubbed raw at her soul. And did she think that this Ravenhill fellow truly had the answers she was looking for? She thought of the Bible verse he'd tacked to the wall of his tiny cabin, of his shirtsleeve with its missing arm, of his story of grief and pain...

*No, he has no answers.* He'd admitted it to her himself. She turned from the door but then paused before retreating down the steps. Despite all he'd experienced, Ravenhill still seemed to have...

*Hope. He has hope.*

Just as Cecil had said of himself and as she'd witnessed in him.

She gritted her teeth. She had no need for a God she couldn't see, who troubled her, who plagued those who followed Him. *I don't want that kind of hope. It's a fool's hope.*

And yet, even as she thought that, she knew, deep inside, she did. She craved it.

Perhaps it was that knowing that caused her to turn once more and knock on the heavy door. *I'll just say hello. I'll tell him about Grandmother's letter, perhaps, too, and see what he thinks. I'll—*

The opening of the door cut off her thoughts. "Come in, quickly!"

An anxious Ravenhill stood in the small crevice he'd opened, as if ready to shut it if she hesitated.

She did hesitate for just a moment, and Ravenhill took her by the arm, pulling her inside.

The door snapped shut behind her.

---

*It would only be polite to stop in and tell Edna that I'm here to watch the storm.* Cecil reasoned as Ginger plodded her way along the muddy path. Jed Stuart's directions had been right-on, and Cecil could identify Scarlet Ridge Farm's unusually tall maple trees up ahead. A small cabin and ramshackle outbuildings greeted him. A thin trail of smoke streamed from the chimney.

He scarcely admitted that he hoped that Edna would like to watch along with him... faint as that hope was. If she was the sort of girl – woman – who liked to watch a rainstorm, not minding a good soaking, well, then Cecil's determination to get to know Edna Sue O'Connell better only would increase – that much he knew.

A scrawny, hunched woman answered his knock. "What do ya want?" she groused, pulling her shawl up over her head, despite the fact that he, not she, was the one getting rained upon.

He smiled. "I'm Cecil Gaunt, ma'am. I'm a friend of Edna Sue, and—"

A bark escaped the woman's tight lips, startling Cecil. "Now I know you're pullin' my leg, sonny. Edna Sue ain't got no friends. Ornery as a porcupine that done met with a fox kit, that one is."

Feisty, surely, and hurting too, though she tried to cover it up, but ornery? No, Cecil wouldn't describe her as that. But he decided not to argue with the woman. "Could you tell her I'm here, ma'am?"

Good thing he didn't mind the rain because this woman didn't appear to be inviting him inside anytime soon. Cecil pulled his collar up to prevent the rain from dripping off his hat and onto his neck.

"Can't."

He forced the frown from his face. "Why not?" he asked pleasantly.

"She ain't here. Took off this afternoon on that fool mule, traipsing off who-knows-where. Like the devil in the Book of Job – going to-and-fro, making mischief, 'stead of keeping at home where she could do her sick daddy some good and help me some, too."

"Are you Edna Sue's mother?"

"Her ma?" Disdain planted itself on the woman's craggy features. "Do I look old enough for that, sonny?"

Never one to tell a lie, Cecil decided that the woman must have meant her question redundantly. He waited for her to elaborate.

"I'm her stepmother," the woman announced. "Her ma's been in the ground these twenty years or more."

"Ah. Well, I'm sorry I've wasted your time, ma'am—" A sharp cough from cabin's interior cut off Cecil's words.

"Be there directly, Caleb," the woman called and, without another word, began to close the door on Cecil.

But the wracking cough had spurred Cecil's compassion, always close to the surface. "Did you say that your husband is ill?" He placed a hand on the door to keep her from shutting it.

She scowled up at him. "Yeah, real sick. Edna didn't wanna get Doc Casey up here, and I ain't in no frame to fetch him myself."

"I'll go." Even as he said it, Cecil winced inwardly as he thought of what Edna's reaction would surely be if she returned to find that Cecil had brought the unwanted Doc Casey to tend her father. He internally shrugged. Well, Edna would just have to reckon with it. From the sounds of it, her father had a terrible cold… or worse.

"You'd do that?" The woman visibly softened, her mouth dropping open. "Rain's a-coming down terrible fierce."

"I like the rain," Cecil answered honestly. "And I've got a horse. If the doctor's at home, I should return within a couple of hours."

"Can't pay ya nothing." The woman's squint threatened him.

"I don't want to be paid, Mrs. O'Connell. It's a kindness for a friend."

# 11

"I apologize for pulling you in like that, but Matilda hates storms," Ravenhill explained, dropping his hold on Edna's upper arm. "I'm always afraid she's going to run out the door when one comes. She goes out of her mind with fear."

"I see that." Beneath the table, the little mutt shook like a Model T from the last century. Edna Sue raised her eyes and glanced around the room. "What in the world are you doing?" Piles of books and odds-and-ends of living had been pulled off Ravenhill's shelves and out of his cupboards. A few crates and cardboard boxes stood half-filled in the center of the floor.

The man smiled. "I'm packing up."

Her heart seized, a slow panic squeezing it. She'd just barely gotten to know him, and now he was leaving, lock, stock, and barrel. "But why? I… I thought that there was nothing left for you in the world."

He stared at the book he'd picked up, smoothing its cover with his thumb. "Perhaps not, Miss O'Connell, but I still must go. I have sat in the dust long enough, so to speak. I have sought the Lord, and He has answered me."

*He has answered me…* Wasn't that just what Edna had longed for, long ago when she yet believed that God would answer her? That He *could* answer her? That He *cared* to answer? "But I thought you said…What…What did He say?"

she asked through dry lips.

Ravenhill met her gaze. "Nothing."

"Nothing?" She gave a sarcastic half-smile. "I'm afraid that I don't think much of your *answer*, then, Mr. Ravenhill."

"He didn't need to tell me why I'd suffered, Miss O'Connell. You see, as I told you before, I realized that He Himself is the answer to our resounding cries of *why, why, why*. In His face, all our questions are laid to rest at last. He Himself was – is the answer I sought."

She frowned, heart and mind twisted in confusion.

"Here." He reached with his good hand for a pocket-sized book remaining on the fireplace mantle. "I'm very pleased that you stopped by. I wanted to give you this." He held the book out to her.

"It's a Bible," she stated, keeping her arms crossed. "I don't need that. I don't want that." Its cover repelled her, for she knew it contained the words of a God who had hurt her without repentance.

But he continued to hold it out to her. "Please, take it for friendship's sake, Miss O'Connell."

*For friendship's sake...* The phrase softened her heart, spring rain upon hard ground. Almost apart from her will, she accepted the book from him. The small leather volume felt heavy in her hands. "Are you returning to the city?" she asked, anxious to change the subject.

He nodded. "Yes. I have a brother there with whom I may live for a time."

"I see."

"He is sending one of our mutual friends to collect my things. Matilda and I will leave tomorrow." He paused and pointed to one of the boxes. "I wonder if you might be interested in taking these volumes for the library in Willow Hollow?"

Edna's breath caught as she looked into the crate he indicated. A dozen books lined it, their gilded spines winking at her in the lamplight. "Dickens... Thackeray... Hardy...

Eliot." She touched the author's names as she read them, then glanced up at Ravenhill. "Are you sure? These are worth a lot of money," she added bluntly.

"The joy they will bring to others on this mountain is worth much more to me than their temporal value. I know that you, of all people, will understand that."

She swallowed the lump that rose in her throat at his high praise. "Thank you, Mr. Ravenhill."

Silence stretched between them for a long moment, and then she shook off her reverie. "Do you think I could come back for them? I'm afraid that in the rain…"

"Certainly."

"Thank you." She swept her eyes around the cabin once more. A tide rose in her breast, too strong for her to hold back as she met Ravenhill's strong and gentle gaze. "I am glad that I met you, Mr. Ravenhill, though we do not agree on everything. And… And… thank you for this, too. I don't know how much good it will do me, but I know that you mean well," she added, indicating the Bible she had placed in the pocket of her trousers.

He smiled and then stretched out his hand. "Good-bye, Miss O'Connell. May God go with you, and may you find Him indeed."

She ground her teeth against the tears that rose to her eyes and shook his hand. "Good-bye, Mr. Ravenhill."

Unable to speak further, she turned to the door and opened it to a veil of rain. Lightning flashed, illuminating the twilight with the clarity of midday. She stepped back into the safety of the cabin. "Perhaps I should wait a few…" Edna began, but thunder drowned out her words just as a black-and-white flash darted past her.

"Matilda!"

Cecil trailed close on the heels of Doc Casey as they approached the O'Connells' door. Half-smiling, he pulled his collar up closer around his neck. True, he did like stormy weather, but this downpour, combined with the thunder and lightning ricocheting in every direction made even Cecil want to seek shelter as quickly as possible – a place to watch the storm in safety!

Ahead of him, Doc Casey pounded the door once before lifting the latch and walking right inside. Cecil followed him.

Ruthie stood from where she sat beside the sick man's bed. One hand grabbed at her lower back as she did so. "Ain'tcha ever heard of waiting for a body to open the door 'fore ya walz in, pretty as ya please?"

"Ruthie, that rain's fixin' to drown a man. Now, how's Caleb doing?" Doc Casey asked, moving toward the bed.

*Where's Edna?* Cecil wished he could ask the question aloud, but given the seriousness of Doctor O'Connell's illness, he hesitated to distract either Ruthie or the doctor. *Is she in the barn?*

"I…I'll take care of the horses," he finally uttered and moved toward the door.

"Iffen you're gonna do that, will ya milk the goats while you're at it? I ain't got no time to do it yet, and night's fast fallin'," explained Ruthie.

"Of course," answered Cecil slowly. Milking the goats held no problem for him; he'd grown up on a small homestead. He couldn't keep the question from escaping his lips, though. "Why doesn't Miss O'Connell do that? Isn't she out in the barn?"

A snort burst from the woman's thin lips. "Not that I know of, she ain't. Never came back from her ride earlier."

His eyes darted toward the greased paper covering the windows. The rain lashed against it. "But the storm… She's out in this?"

Ruthie shrugged. "Ain't my concern. She's a growed-up gal. She's gotta learn to take care of herself one o' these days. I just hope she minded my warning not to go a-visiting that

Ravenhill man again."

Cecil stared at her, wordless for several seconds. "You'll have to milk the goats, ma'am." He limped to the door, donning his sopping hat. "I must find her."

"What? You'll catch your death goin' out again in this. Noxious vapors in the valleys. Or you'll get struck by lightning. It happens, ya know. Happened to my granddaddy. He weren't never the same after that, and I'm not just a-meanin' that he got himself a twitchy eye for the rest of his days!"

Cecil didn't stay to listen to any more. Catching up the reins of Doc Casey's horse, he staggered toward the little barn, where he released it into a stall before removing its tack as quickly as he could. A minute or two of rubbing down its wet coat with a handful of straw had to suffice before he threw an old blanket over its back. "Sorry, old fellow. The doc is sure to tend to you better in a little while."

Securing the barn's door, Cecil lurched across the yard again as quickly as his bad leg could move him. He mounted Ginger, feeling the wetness of the saddle soak into any dry square inch left of his trousers. *Where do I go, Lord?* His mind reeled, numb with panic. *She could be anywhere, anywhere at all!*

For a split second, the helplessness so overwhelmed him that he nearly gave up before he started. *If I don't go, who will? No one.* The thought frightened him into grasping at the last threads of his fast-escaping courage. Straightening in the saddle, he gave a cluck of his tongue to Ginger and a firm tap of his heels to her sides. She obliged him by moving forward at a slow-as-cold-molasses walk.

Despite his need to find Edna Sue as quickly as possible, he knew that he should be thankful for Ginger's pace. The fast-accumulating mud could break a horse's leg if the rider wasn't careful – or even if he was. Cecil blinked in the driving rain; it was all he could do to see ten feet in front of him.

And, as darkness fell over the hills, he knew he would be

able to see even less.

*Ravenhill.* Edna Sue's stepmother had mentioned that she hoped Edna hadn't gone to see that man.

Which – from Cecil's knowledge of Edna Sue – meant that she probably had. *Stubborn mule of a woman!*

He wouldn't have her any other way.

*Show me, Lord. Show me where this Ravenhill lives. And protect Edna Sue.*

---

The branches, nearly-unseen whips in the growing darkness, smacked Edna in the face. "Matilda!" Her voice emerged as a whisper, choked by the fear that gripped her.

"Stay with me! You don't know this area of the mountain well," Ravenhill called over his shoulder, a few feet ahead of her.

"If we split up, we'll find her twice as fast," Edna argued, rubbing her cheek where a particularly nasty branch had sliced at it. Her hand came away moist with blood.

"She may not come to your voice. When Matilda panics, there's no telling what she will do. I've had this dog for two years, and her fear of thunderstorms has not abated."

Edna dug her handkerchief out of her pocket and pressed it against her cheek. *It's smarter to split up. Of course the dog will come to me. She knows me.*

"Keep your eyes down. I know a man who lost one of his to a wayward branch in a storm like this."

Edna Sue nodded as they came to a fork in the barely-discernible trail. "I'll take the left, you take the right."

"We should stay together. I—"

But Edna already headed down the left-hand path. "If I can't find her, I will meet you back at the cabin."

# 12

She'd told him that she followed Sugar Creek nearly all the way. Cecil burrowed his neck deeper into his collar and urged methodical Ginger forward along the muddy bank. He pushed away thoughts that flashed into his mind of Edna Sue lying somewhere, struck by an errant bolt of lightning or with her mule – normally such a surefooted animal – fallen on top of her, its leg broken by the fast-forming, treacherous mud. *Lord, You control every lightning bolt. Guide every step of that mule. Bring her to safety. Help me to find her. My hope is in You.*

A light glimmered through the twilight. At first, Cecil thought he'd imagined it, but then he realized that the light moved toward him. *A lantern.* "Hello!" he called and reined in Ginger, aware that he might be trespassing – a dangerous thing in these mountains.

"Hullo!" came back a young boy's voice. "You're on Holcomb land, mister! State your business and git a move on."

Having come within several feet of Cecil, the boy raised the lantern to shine it in his face. Cecil blinked in the brightness. "I'm looking for Miss O'Connell."

"The bookwoman?" The harshness faded out of the boy's voice, replaced by wonder.

"Yes," Cecil replied eagerly. "The horseback librarian.

I'm a friend of hers. I understand that she might have come this way earlier today, and, with this storm, I thought she possibly would have had trouble returning."

The boy reached up a hand to scratch his rain-soaked hair. "Yeah, she come this way today, but she didn't stop. Ain't her usual day to, I reckon. She headed up the mountain, toward the Ravenhill place. But I wouldn't go up there, mister, if I was ya. That Ravenhill – He's a funny fella, so they say. Hain't met him myself."

"If I did want to go up there, would I just…?"

"Foller the crick," finished the boy. "But I wouldn't if I was—"

"Much obliged. Thank you, son."

*Thank You, Lord.*

---

Had the storm increased in intensity? The branches danced helter-skelter above Edna Sue's head whenever she dared to raise her face, risking, as Ravenhill had warned her, losing an eye. The wind-blown rain, too, made looking up very unpleasant, so she mostly kept her squinted gaze on the ground ahead of her. She remembered the small flashlight she'd had the sense to grab from her saddlebag and to put into her pocket. She drew it out and flicked it on now.

"Matilda!" she called, her voice gaining courage with the flashlight. If she'd been a praying woman… But she wasn't. She'd left that behind years ago. *It's all on me now.* Stumbling over fallen branches, pushing her wet hair away from her eyes, losing her hat…

Then she heard it: a whine. Edna Sue froze for one heartbeat.

There it was again! "Matilda!" she called out, rushing downhill through the wood, through piles of last year's fallen leaves, huddled together against the storm's blast.

Another whine, and then a sharp little bark.

*And Ravenhill thought she wouldn't come to me!* "Umph!" With a grunt, she slipped on a wet rock, coming down flat on her face and hands. Barely stopping to gain back her breath, Edna pushed herself back to her feet and retrieved the flashlight from where it had rolled, snug against the base of a windswept tree. She swished the beam before her, taking in the huge boulder outcropping that loomed over the path ahead. As the rocks rose toward the sky, they grew wider, rather than narrower, as was often the case in these Appalachians, leaving space at their bases where the ground had eroded, forming clefts between the base and the soil.

Another whine. Edna Sue tempered her excitement. Shining a bright light in the dog's face would only frighten her. Instead, she edged the light near where she'd heard the sound, and in the dim halo, saw exactly who she'd been looking for: Matilda, huddled within one of the deepest clefts.

She shook her head. "You poor thing." Slowly, she approached the dog from the side, knowing how skittish an animal out-of-its-mind with fear could be. Reaching the point of the outcropping where she could no longer stand upright, she crouched down and edged her way into the cleft.

Matilda looked at her from the sides of her eyes, whites showing, ears flattened back. The dog's soaked fur trembled with each rumble of thunder.

Glad to be out of the storm, even if it meant she had to squat on a patch of mud, Edna Sue paused for a moment before taking any action with the dog. She shook her head, feeling the drip-drip-drip of the rainwater draining from her hair. "You silly dog. You had no idea how safe you were in that cabin with Ravenhill, did you? Instead, you had to run away from him, into the storm."

Matilda only turned her head a quarter of an inch at Edna's voice. Slowly, Edna edged a little closer to the dog. She needed to get her arms around the mutt without frightening her into running again...

"Gotcha," she murmured as she gently put a hand on the dog's far shoulder. The dog showed no sign of being more or less afraid, so Edna firmly grasped the dog in her arms. Matilda suddenly wiggled and thrashed, but Edna held on. "Ravenhill!" she called at the top of her lungs. "Ravenhill!" She struggled to move from beneath the outcropping without having the use of her hands – an almost impossible task while holding onto a squirming dog whose strength seemed to have multiplied with its fear.

"I'm coming! Keep calling out!"

Relief poured over Edna at the sound of Ravenhill's voice – and not too far away, it seemed to her. His right-hand path must have rejoined the left-hand one she'd taken. "I found her! We're here – near the rocks." She hoped that he would know what she meant, being so familiar with the wooded area near his cabin.

Thunder boomed. Matilda turned her head, burying it into Edna's side. "He's here – He's almost here," she told the dog, an unaccustomed tenderness rising in her chest.

In the crackle of lightning, she saw Ravenhill making his way downhill, only a dozen yards away. The brilliance lit up the woods as though it was midday for one moment. A relieved smile split Ravenhill's bearded face as he stumbled his way forward. "Hold onto her. I'm co—"

A groaning thunder of noise – different from any Edna Sue had heard during the storm thus far – snapped through the air around them, cutting off Ravenhill's words. Edna looked up as best as she could while crouched in the cleft of the rock outcropping, but she couldn't make out the source of the noise. "What—"

*Thrash!* A giant, dark blanket of wet leaves fell before her face, and the realization flashed into her mind that a nearby tree had split... and headed their way. Despite her usual self-control, Edna screamed as a branch whacked her face. She clutched the dog against her to protect it from this unlooked-for onslaught.

A moment concluded it. She reached a hand up and felt the jagged rock ceiling. Darkness stretched out on either side of her. And, before her smarting face, her hand met the tangled branches of what felt like a huge oak tree. It had shut her and the dog into the cleft.

*My flashlight.* Still holding onto Matilda, she fumbled for it and with a sinking heart, realized that she had no idea where she'd dropped it when she'd screamed. She gulped for a breath to relieve her aching chest. "Ravenhill!" she called.

But no one answered her.

"Ravenhill!" Her heart threatened to pound its way out of the prison of her ribs. Outside the black trap in which she found herself, the storm's intensity grew. "Ravenhill!"

The dog whined and licked at her face.

*What am I going to do?*

"Ravenhill! Ravenhill! Ravenhill!" She screamed the name, panic skittering through her veins. She had lost control; she knew it and no longer cared. Something had happened to Ravenhill. *I am in a hole in the rock with a dog and am never going to get out!*

Her mind ran. No one knew where she was, not really. Only Ruthie had an inkling, and Edna Sue knew that her stepmother would not bother to send anyone after her, at least not for days. *What have I done? This is such a mess.* Her screams trickled away into weeping as helplessness covered her, a smothering blanket. *There's no one to help. No one…*

There in that cleft, only One crouched with Edna and that little black-and-white dog. So alone, she could not ignore His presence. Dare she admit? She *needed* His presence.

"Oh, God…"

She had few words but those as she wept through the long hours of darkness and storm.

# 13

He had lost his way; he might as well admit it. Cecil blinked away the driving rain and drew Ginger to a halt. The patient beast blew out a breath. "Sorry, old girl," he muttered, laying a chilled hand to her wet neck. *Help me find the way, Lord.*

But what if he didn't find her? What if he had truly lost himself in these seemingly never-ending woods?

*Then please, dear God, be near to her. Hide her in the cleft of the rock.*

The wind began to die away; the rain dwindled, slowly, reluctantly; the thunder faded. It had nearly passed when Edna Sue lifted her tear-soaked face from where she'd buried it in Matilda's neck fur. The darkness of night still covered them, made deeper by their position in the natural cage that hemmed them in on every side.

*Singing... Is that singing in the darkness?* Unbelieving, she held her breath so that she could hear the faint noise better.

It was Ravenhill. She was sure of it. The soft voice continued,

*"A wonderful Saviour is Jesus my Lord*

*He taketh my burden away*
*He holdeth me up and I shall not be moved*
*He giveth me strength as my day.*
*He hideth my soul in the cleft of the rock*
*That shadows a dry, thirsty land*
*He hideth my life in the depths of His love*
*And covers me there with His hand*
*And covers me there with His hand..."*

She found her own voice, choked as it was with joy. "Ravenhill! We're in here. We can't get out because of the tree."

There was silence for a moment, then Ravenhill answered, "I know, Miss O'Connell. I-I can't get to you."

Her heart sank. She remembered how he was missing an arm. Of course he couldn't pull away this tree by himself. "Perhaps if I push on this side..." she began, scrambling to think of a way of escape.

"No. No, it's best to wait until someone comes." His voice sounded weary. "Someone will come."

"How do you know?" she persisted. "Wouldn't it be better to—"

"Someone will come, Miss O'Connell. I see the morning star; it will be light soon." He paused. "I will continue singing so that you remember that you're not alone here."

His singing trickled through the heavy branches that blocked her from escape, and she realized that, for once, the words to the old hymn soothed rather than angered her.

*"A wonderful Saviour is Jesus my Lord*
*A wonderful Saviour to me*
*He hideth my soul in the cleft of the rock*
*Where rivers of pleasure I see..."*

It seemed a long time later that the dawn began to powder

the snatches of sky that Edna Sue could glimpse between the fallen tree's branches. The light renewed Edna's spirit, despite the fact that help had not yet arrived. She laid her head against quieted Matilda and closed her eyes, comforted by Ravenhill's continued singing:

*"When clothed in His brightness*
*Transported I rise*
*To meet Him in clouds of the sky*
*His perfect salvation, His wonderful love*
*I'll shout with the millions on high*
*He hideth my soul in the cleft of the rock*
*That shadows a dry, thirsty land*
*He hideth my life in the depths of His love*
*And covers me there with His hand..."*

Something had changed in her heart, provoked by the example of Ravenhill, birthed by the powerlessness she'd known during last night's storm. To her own astonishment, Edna Sue recognized the trusting faith of her childhood had begun to return to the nest of her soul.

"Edna Sue! Edna Sue!"

She didn't know if the calling woke her or if it was Matilda's struggle to rise, having tired of being used as a pillow. Edna shook the haziness of sleep from her head, sucked in a breath, and opened her eyes.

Light filtered through the branches that imprisoned her, yet it was the stronger light of day, rather than that of dawn. Her back to Edna Sue, Matilda barked, then looked at Edna and whimpered.

"Edna Sue O'Connell! Answer if you can hear me!"

*Cecil.* Her heart tumbled through her chest upon hearing

his voice. How had he known? How had he come, with his leg the way it was?

"Edna!"

Scrambling forward toward the branches barring her way, she opened her mouth to answer but only a croak emerged. Swallowing, she tried again. "I'm here! Cecil, I'm here. We're trapped behind the fallen tree."

She heard the snapping of underbrush and imagined that he must be rushing her way.

"Are you all right, Edna?"

Her heart warmed at the concern in his voice, a sensation she had not permitted herself to feel for many years. "Y-yes, we're all right."

"And who's with you?"

She smiled at Matilda, who gave a sloppy kiss to her scratched cheek. "Just the dog. Mr. Ravenhill is somewhere nearby, though." She suddenly realized that she had not heard Ravenhill's singing since she'd awoken. "Unless he went for help."

She heard Cecil move around for a few moments, then pause. "I-I need to get your mule up at Ravenhill's place. I can't move that tree by myself. Will you be all right if I leave? You're no more than five minutes from the cabin."

"Yes, we'll be fine." She stroked Matilda's head. "We'll be just fine."

# 14

Hours ago, Cecil had finally arrived at Ravenhill's cabin at last just as the sun rose over the horizon, dissolving the last of the storm clouds. His heart had sunk as he'd surveyed the door swinging wide open, the half-packed boxes, and Molly standing rather impatiently in the small shed. He'd not permitted his mind to deliberate long, though, but had left exhausted Ginger to Molly's company while he continued on foot.

His mistake, he now realized, had been going north first. If he'd headed south immediately, he would have stumbled upon them within a few minutes, most likely. As it was, his wristwatch told him that it was nearly eight-o-clock in the morning. If only he had gotten there sooner...

Now, drawing upon the last percentage of energy he had left, Cecil dragged himself up the front steps of Ravenhill's porch and deposited his heavy burden gently on the bed.

*How will I tell Edna Sue?* He sucked in a breath. *Did she...did she love him?* Staring down at the body, he knew that the bloody head wound surely had taken the man's life in the end.

Shaking out a soft blanket, he carefully covered the body. Though he had not known Ravenhill, every creature deserved dignity in death.

"Heave – Ho!" With a final burst of strength, Molly pulled away the thick trunk, her mule muscles working hard.

Freedom! Matilda burst from the opened prison, with Edna Sue close behind, crawling on all fours through muck and cutting her hands afresh on the sharp rocks.

Masculine hands clasped her forearms, drawing her to her feet. She winced at the tightness of her leg muscles as she came face-to-face with Cecil Gaunt, her unlikely rescuer if there ever was one.

"Are you hurt?" he asked, concern flooding his voice. His hands came to her elbows, better supporting her.

She realized that he had seen her grimace. "No, my muscles stiffened from crouching for so long." She smiled, and her heart knew lightness at the genuineness of it. "Thank you, Mr. Gaunt."

His eyes moved over her face, as if… as if he couldn't look at her enough. Yet how could that be? "Edna Sue, you are a sight for sore eyes," he said at last.

"I'm sure I am." She shook her head. The tenderness in his eyes – well, it scared her yet. "Look at me: mud, scratches, blood."

"You don't see what I see."

"And what's that?" she asked before thinking.

"A beautiful woman of courage and perseverance."

Her heart caught on the bramble of affection in Cecil's voice – caught and yet struggled to be free of the fearful, unaccustomed thing. She stepped back from his hands so gently supporting her and stumbled on her own shaky legs.

"Come on, let's get you back to town. I have a horse up at the cabin if you're able to ride Molly," said Cecil, as if she hadn't ignored his remark.

"I wonder if we should wait at the cabin, just in case Ravenhill returns with help." She would hate for the older man to panic – though he really didn't seem to be the panicking sort – if he found her and the dog gone from the rock outcropping *and* absent from the cabin. She forced herself to move toward the path that led north to the cabin, the dog at her heels.

"I need to tell you something."

The seriousness of Cecil's tone brought Edna's feet to a halt. She turned, dread rising. "What is it?" *Please, please don't make a declaration of love right now.* Their friendship, just budding, would be ruined and—

"It's about Ravenhill."

"Ravenhill?" She stopped, her heart thudding loud.

Cecil met her eyes, and the compassion in his gaze told her what his lips had not yet done.

"He's dead," she stated quietly. Her hand reached down to pat Matilda.

Cecil swallowed and nodded. "Yes."

"Where is he?" She looked around. "Last night, he sang through the darkness. For hours. He wouldn't go for help. Now I know why." She sniffed, tears pushing at the back of her eyes.

Cecil stepped toward her. Above their heads, a nuthatch called from high in the pines. "I brought him back to the cabin when I went to get Molly. He… He was banged up pretty badly on his head, Edna. I didn't want you to see him like that."

She sucked in a breath of mountain air, its fresh, woody scent grounding her. "Thank you, Mr. Gaunt. I know that couldn't have been easy for you, with your leg."

Without waiting to hear his response, she turned to head up the path toward the cabin again, but she found that it looked so much longer now. So much more uphill. Weariness draped every inch of her body and soul. The tears that had pressed moments before now demanded freedom.

And she was very tired of holding them in.

She stood, back to him, strong and capable... and now so burdened by sorrow. Could it be that she would allow him to carry some of the weight? *Lord, help me.* For Cecil knew he hadn't the strength in himself to face his own sorrows, let alone that of another soul.

When her feet remained stationary and her shoulders drooped, Cecil stepped forward. Pain shot through his leg as it hadn't for years, but he pushed through it, stopping only when the back of Eda Sue's mud-caked head was inches from him. Gently, as he would with a wild animal accidentally caught in a trap, Cecil touched Edna's shoulder, urging her to turn toward him.

She resisted for only a moment and then, almost before he could reckon how it had occurred, Edna leaned against him, weeping. He placed his arms around her, holding her to himself.

Soon, though, she pushed against his chest, drawing back. "I'm sorry. I don't know what came over me," she mumbled, wiping her nose on her sleeves. "I'm sorry. My handkerchief is rather useless at this point, I'm afraid."

"It's all right, Miss O'Connell. You know, my mother says that tears are one of the ways God cleanses the soul. Don't be afraid of tears – unless they're ones of self-pity. I've cried too many of those myself and know they rarely help matters," he added, his lips quirking in sympathy.

She ducked her head but then looked back up at him, a smile softening her lips, too. "Thank you, again. Ravenhill's death hit me hard. Harder this morning, I think, than it would have yesterday morning."

Cecil's heart clenched. "I'm sorry. I know that you... cared for him."

She tilted her head, and Cecil wondered if she realized how charming she appeared with her crooked, smudged spectacles and unkempt hair. "I did care for him, but not in the way that I believe you're assuming."

Was it wrong that his spirit lifted at those words?

She went on. "He was... like a spiritual father to me, though I only knew him such a short while. He helped me to begin to see the circumstances of my life differently. To begin to see God's ways differently. He helped me to begin to believe again in the only One who can give me hope – as have you, Mr. Gaunt." She sniffled. "I will miss him."

She lifted her eyes then and met his with a sad but peaceful smile – a smile that gave Cecil the courage to take her battered hand in his. He held his breath, but she kept her hand in the embrace of his as they made their way back to Ravenhill's cabin, Matilda at their heels all the way.

---

As they came into cabin's yard, Edna gently pulled her hand from Cecil's. In her heart and mind, she knew that it didn't belong there – yet. The sudden absence of it in hers lingered as a sweet ache.

"What about the dog?"

At Cecil's question, Edna looked at Matilda. The creature rushed around the yard, nose to the ground, tail at half-mast. *Poor thing; she's searching for her master.* "I'll take her," Edna heard herself say and knew that her own expression must be as surprised – and pleased – as Cecil's appeared to her.

He nodded. "My horse is in the stable. I rented it from Pastor Stuart's livery. When I return it, I can tell him about Ravenhill. Unless you would like to, that is. I know that he was your friend."

She shook her head. "It's kind of you. Please, you go ahead."

"Do you know if he had any family?"

She hesitated. "His wife and child were gone. I don't know if he had parents still living. He had a brother with whom he meant to live upon leaving the mountains. And he had a friend who owned the cabin and brought him supplies. He may have letters among his things." She glanced toward the cabin, unable to repress the shudder of sorrow when she thought of Ravenhill's body lying cold in there. "I don't really wish to go inside now, though, and look."

Even as she said it, the last words she'd heard from Ravenhill's mouth returned to her:

*When clothed in His brightness, transported I rise*
*To meet Him in clouds of the sky...*

Even in a seemingly senseless death, Ravenhill's last speech had been one of faith – of eternal hope.

*Oh, living God, forgive me. May that be true of me from this time forward.*

---

They buried him two days later in the churchyard, with Pastor Stuart presiding. Edna had expected no one to come but the Stuarts, Cecil, and herself, yet a sizeable crowd gathered – no doubt out of curiosity about the mysterious one-armed mountain man who had died by what they called an act of God.

"I didn't know Mr. Ravenhill," Pastor Stuart said to Edna as she turned to leave the churchyard. "But Mr. Gaunt tells me that you were a good friend to him."

Edna lifted her eyes to meet Pastor Stuart's, feeling somewhat awkward with this man at whom she had often sniffed in disdain because of his profession. "Yes," she agreed, smoothing her skirt. She so rarely wore a dress that when she did, she felt self-conscious – an unusual sensation indeed for her.

"I'm sorry, then, for your loss."

"Thank you."

"Someone has contacted his family – if he has them?"

Edna nodded. She had been unable to bring herself to return to the cabin yet. Perhaps someday. "I believe Mr. Gaunt said that he will take care of those matters. He wishes to return to Possum Valley soon, anyway, to explore the possibility of starting a school for the children there." Indeed, she and Cecil had spoken of as much on the long way down the mountain yesterday, and her heart, cleared of so much of its bitterness and confusion, had begun to glow with excitement at the prospect, regardless of the many obstacles that remained in the way.

Pastor Stuart's face split with a smile. "Oh, that's good news, indeed. I've been concerned in prayer for those children and their families for some time."

"We don't know if it will get off the ground yet," Edna Sue cautioned.

"Still, I'm glad to hear it."

"As am I." She turned to go, but the minister's question stopped her.

"And your daddy? I heard that he was poorly."

She saw true concern shine in Pastor Stuart's eyes, and another piece of ice melted away from her soul. "He's doing better, thank you. He's sitting up again, and there's been talk of bringing him outside on one of these nice days – getting him some fresh air."

The minister smiled. "I'm very glad to hear that, Miss O'Connell. We'll keep praying for him."

"Thank you." She paused. "Well, good morning, Pastor Stuart. I will see you in church on Sunday," she added, a little mischief playing in her heart.

Shock and delight battled for victory on the preacher's face. "Well, that's fine news, too! I'll look forward to seeing you there, Miss O'Connell."

With a nod and smile, she left the churchyard before Cecil, who lingered nearby, could catch up with her.

# 15

*Two Weeks Later*

A sight across Main Street completely absorbed Cecil's attention as he limped out of the General Store: Edna Sue O'Connell, dressed neatly in a brown suit, stepped from the bus that ran from Willow Hollow to the city. One of her gloved hands clasped the handle of a valise; the other, a leash which tethered Matilda.

He swallowed the nervousness that pushed up his throat. So. She had returned from New York City, so many miles away, much larger even than the little city nearby that the folks of Willow Hollow wondered at.

He watched as she dusted off her clothing and adjusted the dog's leash. Then – then, she raised her eyes and met his gaze. She stood quite still for a moment before raising a hand in greeting.

He lifted his own in response and prepared to start toward her, but she turned away, striding toward the outskirts of town, where the trail toward Scarlet Ridge Farm began.

It was not enough. He wanted more.

Off to Pastor Stuart's livery he went.

All of the valley below Scarlet Ridge stretched before her. Edna Sue edged near the drop-off and lowered herself until she sat with her legs crisscrossed, glad for the trousers she'd changed into once she'd returned to the farm.

Her eyes caught on a crimson bird dipping in flight as it made its way from one giant pine to another – a northern cardinal. How gracefully it made its way through the groundless air, trusting to the wings and wind currents its Creator had given it. So she, too, would hope – not in herself and her circumstances any longer, but in Him who had created her and permitted them. He would uphold her in His gracious hand and bring her at last to His own great nest.

"Miss O'Connell."

She startled at the unexpected voice and looked over her shoulder. Mr. Gaunt. *Cecil.* Her heart fluttered like that of a flighty sixteen-year-old girl rather than that of a sensible woman approaching her forties. Unsettled at the anticipatory excitement that stole over her, Edna switched her gaze back to the valley below. "Hello, Mr. Gaunt. How... How have you been?"

A pause. "Well." He limped to her side and eased himself to sit beside her. "Where's Matilda?"

Edna couldn't help but smile at the dog's name. "In the cabin with Daddy. They've become quite attached to each other. I would have left her here when I went to New York, but I wasn't sure that Ruthie could handle a dog with Daddy still recovering from his illness."

"You could have left Matilda with me. I would have enjoyed caring for her."

Was Cecil miffed with her? Edna Sue was tempted to sneak a glance at him from the corner of her eye. She wouldn't blame him if he was; she'd snuck away without telling anyone about her trip except for Ruthie and Daddy. Oh, of course, Curt Armstrong and the library ladies knew, too, because they had needed to adjust their routes to account for her absence.

She'd be honest. She was an independent woman and sometimes needed to do things on her own. If Cecil didn't like that... well, it was best that they both find out now. "I know that you think I should have told you that I was leaving town for a few days—"

"Not *should have*," he put in quietly. "Would have wanted to, I'd have liked to think, that's all."

Her mouth hung open, wordless for a moment.

"You see, Miss O'Connell – Edna Sue," he went on, his own gaze on the treeline yonder, "I think that if folks care about one another, they want to confide in each other. They want to share themselves – where they're going, what they're thinking and feeling – with one another. That's all."

Hm. Well, that was something to consider. "I haven't... confided, as you put it, in anyone for so long, I suppose that I have forgotten how important it can be... for friendships."

The soreness still stretched between them a bit, though lightened by her confession. She turned to face his profile. "Would it be all right with you if I confided in you now, Mr. Gaunt – Cecil?"

A smile grew on his lips as he met her gaze. "I would consider it an honor if you wish to."

"I do." Her heart began to drum as she spoke aloud for the first time what decisions she had come to on her trip to New York, her long-time cherished dream. "A few weeks ago, my grandmother wrote to me. At eighty, she wished to mend the fences, so to speak, between us and name me as her heir in her will. She is a very wealthy woman," she clarified so that Cecil would understand that she spoke of inheriting a fortune, not a three-legged milking stool.

His eyes widened, his jaw tightened, but he remained silent.

"Her stipulation: that I return to the city, to her home. She would provide the money for someone to care for Daddy and Ruthie here at Scarlet Ridge Farm, something she had refused to do in the past."

Cecil frowned. "Why?"

Edna sighed. "She has been angry with Daddy ever since he took Mother and me back to the mountains many years ago, when I was a child. When he had his stroke and Ruthie recalled me to Scarlet Ridge, Grandmother demanded that Daddy return to the city for care permanently. When he and Ruthie refused and I remained with them, Grandmother washed her hands of us all. I hadn't heard from her for a decade."

"It was right for you to stay and care for your father. Surely your grandmother should have seen that."

Edna shrugged. "I can't say. At any rate, I remained here out of duty. Eventually, my bitterness toward Daddy's God, who had called Daddy to these hills and then permitted such terrible things to occur, twisted my love for Daddy into a near-hatred." She gave him a quick glance. "It's not that way anymore, but that's how it was for a long, long time, Cecil."

"Until you met Ravenhill."

"Yes. Ravenhill... and you, too. God used both of you in different ways." She turned toward the valley again, and the sight of its vast beauty nearly took away her breath. "Strange how I used to think of this place as a prison, with Daddy and God and Ruthie as my jailors. Anyway, where was I?"

"Your grandmother's condition of returning to the city."

She nodded. "Yes." Edna breathed deeply. "I said that I couldn't do that. Not now."

She couldn't resist glancing over at Cecil just to see the shock on his face. "But why? Why? I thought you wanted..."

"I thought I did." How could she explain all that had occurred in her heart and mind in the last few days and weeks when she didn't even completely understand it all herself? "But I don't anymore. My desires have changed. I want to see the

Possum Valley children get an education now; I can help them with that. I want to see if God will yet restore the years that the locusts of my bitterness have eaten in my relationship with Daddy and even Ruthie. Those things are so much more important than fulfilling the glittery, selfish dreams I once held for myself – and am now learning to release."

He nodded slowly. "And your grandmother?"

Edna straightened her shoulders, remembering Grandmother's reaction to her decision. "She was furious. She ordered me to leave her home." She paused. That rejection had hurt. "But she has changed her mind more than once, so who knows what the future holds?"

Cecil met her gaze, his own smile warming his eyes like a wood fire on a winter's night. Gently yet without hesitation, he reached for her hand, fitting it with his. "I know what I would like for it to hold, though," he stated quietly.

Edna Sue's breath caught at the clear intent of his words. She turned to face him, but he looked out at the valley again and said nothing more for the time.

She tamped down her own impatience to always know the next step ahead and turned her own gaze outward. There was time enough to talk of more. Right now, they would enjoy the view from Scarlet Ridge.

*The Secret Place of Thunder*

# Historical Note: Librarians on muleback? Did it really happen?

In the 1930s, the United States fell into the Great Depression, a severe economic downturn. As part of his response, President Franklin Roosevelt instituted the Works Progress Administration (WPA), which sought to provide employment and opportunity for Americans, especially those in poverty-stricken areas. A WPA project, the Pack Horse Library Program began in the mid-30s with the goal of employing women and spreading literacy in the rural Kentucky Appalachians, an area that the Depression had hit hard.

Each county had several librarians – usually local women (and a few men), who worked out of a small library. Local school boards normally supported the library by providing rent, heat, and electricity (if available), with the understanding that the library would aid the local school with resources. One main librarian usually stayed at the library building itself; he or she was often responsible for sorting and repairing the materials. The other librarians headed out on the trail, packing books and magazines into their saddlebags.

Every librarian (sometimes called a "bookwoman") received a section of the county for which she was held responsible. Each section then was divided into a set of routes. The WPA required the librarians to ride each of their routes twice a month – thus, a bi-weekly rotation – with each librarian riding over one hundred miles a week – uphill and downhill, through swollen creeks and dangerous weather. The librarians provided their own horse or mule and received a monthly salary of $28 – an adequate wage at the time.

The Pack Horse Program attracted attention from schools, churches, and social groups outside the Appalachian area. These groups donated money and materials to the program, which tremendously grew within a year as mountain folk became accustomed to having literature available that opened their eyes to a world outside the Appalachians. In 1943, with the United States' entrance into WWII, the Pack Horse Library Program officially closed, but the legacy of literature which the bookwomen brought to the mountains lived on.

*Hello, reading friends!*

Thank you for coming along to the Appalachian hills of Willow Hollow, Kentucky with me! I hope that you've enjoyed the adventure and that your faith in the Lord Jesus Christ has been expanded, as has mine while I wrote Edna Sue's story.

If you'd like to continue the adventures in Willow Hollow, this novella joins three others as part of a multi-author series, *Librarians of Willow Hollow*. Each book in the series tells the story of one of the town's librarians. Read Lena's story in *A Strand of Hope*, Lillian's in *I Love to Tell the Story*, and Ivory's in *Hearts on Lonely Mountain*. Each book can be read as a stand-alone, though I think you will enjoy every one of them!

Curious about my other books? Stop by my website at: www.aliciagruggieri.com and visit me on Facebook at http://www.facebook.com/AliciaGRuggieri. If you enjoy book giveaways and would like to receive my latest writing/release news and launch team invitations, I would love to connect with you through my newsletter. You can sign up for that on my website.

Lastly, if you have enjoyed this novella, would you leave a short review on your favorite retail site, such as Amazon, and on social media, such as Goodreads? That really helps other readers find books they will love! Thank you!

May the Lord guide and keep you in the hollow of His hand, in the cleft of the Rock, friends.

*In the Cross,*

*Alicia G. Ruggieri*

*2 Corinthians 4:7*

# *Acknowledgments*

Like dwarves, books do not "just spring out of the ground." I'm very thankful for the following people God has provided to help guide *The Secret Place of Thunder* to its publication.

- ❖ My fellow Willow Hollow authors – Amanda, Anita, and Faith – I'm glad we were able to travel these trails together! I'm thankful for the input each of you gave to make this story the best it could be and to fit well with the others in this series.
- ❖ My excellent first readers, who gave me the feedback needed to make Edna's story the best it could be – Londie, Rebekah, and, of course, my book-loving Mama-Bee, and my husband Alex. Thanks for never letting me settle for the mediocre!
- ❖ Those who pray for me and my writing – I can't name you each and all, but your intercession is so greatly appreciated and needed. Thank you!
- ❖ My Lord and Savior, who "He maketh my feet like hinds' feet, and setteth me upon my high places" (Psalm 18:33).

# Amanda Tero

## A Strand of Hope

**Lena Davis is the daughter her mom never wanted.**

But she survived. Through stories. Because books didn't judge. Books weren't angry she was alive. Books never expected her to be anything but who she was.

As she grows up, her beloved library becomes her true home.

So when the library is designated part of President Roosevelt's Packhorse Library Project, Lena is determined to get the job of bringing books to highlanders, believing she'll finally be free of her mom forever.

But earning the trust of highlanders is harder than she imagined, and her passion for books might not be enough to free her from her chains.

### amandatero.com

# Faith Blum

## I Love to Tell the Story

*Her heart is in the right place...*

Bored with her life in Castle Town, Montana, Lillian Sullivan follows her friend's suggestion and joins the horseback librarian program in rural Kentucky. Not only does she anticipate sharing her love of books, but she also wants to spread the gospel among the mountain people.

However, Willow Hollow presents her with one trouble after another and she struggles to step outside her shyness to share the gospel.

What will it take for Lillian to share her love of the Best Story? Can the power of the gospel overcome the shyness of her own heart?

## faithblum.com

# A.M. Heath

## Hearts on Lonely Mountain

*Can two lonely people find more than a fleeting friendship or will a prejudiced town keep them apart?*

When Ivory Bledsoe left the city to minister to the people of the rural mountain town of Willow Hollow, she never expected to be shunned rather than welcomed. Seeing the town as a lost cause, she's eager to return home, but when the bridge leading out of own is washed away during a flood, she finds herself stranded in the last place she wants to be.

Ben Thrasher was content with his quiet life until he met the new librarian. He can't help but be drawn to the friendly and lively Ivory Bledsoe, despite her being at the center of the town's latest superstition. It's only a matter of time until she captures his heart, turning his world upside down in the process.

Has Ivory gotten God's plan for her all wrong or is there still a way she can serve these people? And can Ben ask her to stay in a place where so few are willing to embrace her?

# christianauthoramheath.net

If you enjoyed this book, keep reading for a peek into Alicia G. Ruggieri's novel *The Fragrance of Geraniums*, set in 1930s Rhode Island.

# An Excerpt from

## *The Fragrance of Geraniums*

## *(A Time of Grace, Book 1)*

## by Alicia G. Ruggieri

### September 1934

She tucked a piece of gold behind her ear, nervously twisting the whisper-thin strands from the root to the tip. Her hands – blue veins rivering through the translucent flesh – shook so badly. She held them out from her body, willing them to stop trembling, entreating, pleading with them. But they wouldn't stop shaking, acting as independent entities, outside of Grace's control.

Desperate now, she clasped them together tighter than the knot that tethered the family cow to its post in the barn. Her knuckles turned white from the pressure. The blood began to hammer through her chest, and she tried to remind herself to breathe…

But breathing was the last thing she really was worried about at the moment.

*It's now or never, Grace*, she reminded herself. She tasted blood and realized that she'd clenched her jaw so hard that she'd bit the inside of her mouth without meaning to. Hastily, she ran her tongue over her teeth, just in case.

The auditorium had emptied of other students, like a lunchbox after noon. Its vast ceiling domed over the rows and rows of seats, their wood polished by so many years of parents and students sliding around on the surfaces. *In Memory of Pauline Durferts: 1912* proclaimed the gold plaque above the stage's proscenium arch. Grace couldn't see it in the dim light – Mr. Kinner only had a lamp on now – but she'd read it every time there had been a school assembly last year.

*What would it be like,* Grace often had wondered, *to have a school auditorium named in your honor?* She knew that she would probably never experience that, but wasn't that what secret dreams were for? Grace lived in awe of Pauline Durferts who had the auditorium named after her. Though she wished poor deceased Pauline might have had a more elegant name. Durferts Memorial Auditorium didn't swing off the tongue very prettily... nor did it look so great on the playbills. Grace shrugged. *I suppose, if you have the money to give an auditorium to the high school, it doesn't matter what your last name sounds like.*

She moved down the aisle, silently making her way up to Mr. Kinner. Beneath her blue cardigan, worn so threadbare that she could see her blouse through it in the light, Grace felt her heart clatter loudly. For a moment, she thought that the teacher might hear it. But Mr. Kinner sat with his head turned away from her, seemingly oblivious to Grace's obnoxious heartbeats as she approached him.

*Flop.* Grace froze in the aisle. Her eyes darted toward Mr. Kinner. He hadn't heard; his head still bent over his papers, the piano lamp sending up a glow, illuminating the man like a candle in the darkness. Relieved, Grace crouched down to examine her shoe.

*Where's that elastic?* Grace gritted her teeth and felt about in the darkness. Her fingers came into contact with several sticky substances on the worn floor, including a chunk of old bubblegum. She bit back her disgust and kept inching her way around in circles. *Where is that elastic?* Finally, Grace's fingers touched the rubbery strand. She gave a sigh of relief and scooped it up.

But the elastic band had broken. Not merely fallen off, but totally snapped from where she'd put it to hold her flopping sole on - and to take away some of the disgrace her shoes brought her. The hollow agony of her situation nibbled away at Grace's shaky confidence. She couldn't face Mr. Kinner with such an obviously-broken shoe. She couldn't stand to see the derision or, worse, pity smooth over his handsome college-graduate features as he took in not only her dingy plaid skirt, stockingless legs, and scrappy cardigan but also her flopping shoes. As she'd dressed this morning, she'd hoped against hope that the rubber band might mask the fact that her footwear was so... used up. But it hadn't worked after all.

In the dark, cold auditorium, Grace let one tear press its way past her iron reserve. Then she gathered up her broken dreams, folded them neatly in the drawers of her memory, and turned the key. She silently rose to her feet and turned to leave the assembly room by the same door through which she'd entered.

*Flop. Flop.* Grace froze again. Her shoe was giving her away! Perhaps Mr. Kinner hadn't heard. Perhaps he had immersed himself too entirely in his work to pay any mind to some miscellaneous *flop*...

"Is someone here?" The deep voice, friendly though it was, made Grace nearly choke. She heard the creak of the piano bench and knew that Mr. Kinner had twisted around to look out into the auditorium's blackness. "Hello?"

Grace forced herself to turn. She had thought that her nerves were bad before she'd broken the shoe's rubber band. Now she thought she might really, truly faint. "It's just me, sir," she squeezed out. Her hands went numb. "But I'm going now."

She turned and made it almost to the heavy double exit doors before Mr. Kinner's voice rang out again, cheerfully asking about the shocking thing Grace had actually come here to do:

"Did you want to sign up for something?"

She swallowed and faced him again. My, but the room seemed to have grown every minute she'd been there. She opened her mouth but not a syllable could find its way to her dry tongue, past her stiff teeth. There was nothing for it. She moved down the aisle clumsily, trying to prevent the flop-flopping of her shoe. When she finally reached the piano, Mr. Kinner sat sifting through the stack of papers before him. He smiled up at her. "Grace Picoletti, right?" She nodded and tasted blood in her mouth again. Consciously, she forced her teeth to relax their grip on the inside of her cheek.

"I have the sign-up forms here. Band? No, you don't play an instrument, do you? Theatre?"

He looked up at Grace, who shook her head violently, drawing a smile from him again. "No? What, then?"

Grace swallowed down the lump that felt like cancer in her throat. "Chorus," she managed to breathe out finally, but Mr. Kinner just looked confused.

He hadn't heard. She would have to try again. "Chorus," she forced her voice box to grind out. There, it was done. She felt the sweat cool on her forehead and looked numbly down at her defunct saddle shoes.

"Chorus? Oh, well, what part do you sing?"

Startled, Grace gaped up at him. What did he mean? She had no idea of singing a *part*; she only wanted to be in the chorus, standing as far to the back row as possible. "I... I don't know," she finally stuttered, sure that she looked as foolish as she felt.

Mr. Kinner smiled like he'd been eating molasses cookies, and Grace – in the midst of feeling embarrassed and awkward – found her heart skipping beats. He flipped through the music piled on the piano, selected a single sheet, and set it before him. "Well," he said, eyes on Grace, "do you know *America the Beautiful*?"

Grace nodded. Everyone knew that.

"How about if I play it, and you try to sing along? Just so we can see what your range is." He poised his long fingers expertly over the ivory keys and looked up at her, waiting for her answer.

Grace froze. Sing? In front of Mr. Kinner? Alone, without any other voices to drown hers out?

"Here, I'll get you started." Mr. Kinner tapped his foot a few times and his fingers began to run lightly over the keys, with the same kind of joy she saw her Mama feel when...

But now he was singing in that lovely caramel voice, and he expected her to follow suit! She opened her thin lips, but the notes would not emerge. Mr. Kinner looked over at her encouragingly after the first verse, and Grace tried valiantly once more.

This time, she managed a half-whisper, half-croak for the first few words. Mr. Kinner smiled – Was he making sport or did he like how she sang? Grace tried a few more lines, and Mr. Kinner's lips spread into a wide half-moon as he dropped his hands from the piano and onto his knees. "That was excellent, Grace!" he exclaimed before turning back to the piano, his shining eyes reflecting in the instrument's well-polished surface. Grace turned the color of wild strawberries, confused at the mixture of embarrassment and overpowering pleasure she felt at his compliments.

"I think I'll start you on soprano and go from there. Practice is every Friday after school." Mr. Kinner glanced at his pocket-watch, and the bench squeaked as he rose to his feet with a smile. "I've got to get going now, but you just get this permission slip signed by your parents." He handed her a sheet of mimeographed paper from one of the piles on top of the upright.

Still returning to earth, Grace nearly dropped the permission slip. She clutched at it with her sweaty fingertips. "Thank you," she breathed.

"You're welcome," he returned, grabbing his briefcase from beneath the piano. He clicked off the piano light, and darkness settled into the room, leaving only the light from the partially-open door. "Careful as you exit," he cautioned.

Grace nodded mutely, backing up, holding onto the permission slip for dear life, not paying mind to the flop of her shoe. And of course, that did it. With the sickening knowledge that she was too far gone to do anything about it, Grace stumbled backward in the aisle, clutching helplessly at the empty air. She landed flat on her back, gasping for breath, staring up at the far-off ceiling, desperately pulling her pleated skirt down from where it bunched at her waist.

Before she could regain any composure, though, Mr. Kinner knelt at her side, concern written over his smoothly-shaven face. "Whoa, there. Are you alright?" he asked, hand to her shoulder.

Grace struggled to sit up, and he helped her, holding her elbow gently. She nodded. "I'm... I'm... o-okay," she stammered and scrambled to stand, straightening her skirt and blouse. Her cheek stung where she had hit it on one of the wooden seats, but that was nothing – *nothing* – to the excruciating shame she felt as Mr. Kinner's gaze landed on her shoe. He said nothing, but she saw the surprise, then understanding flood his eyes in the two seconds that he spent looking downwards.

She couldn't bear it. Grace turned and ran. She would not wait to see the pity that surely would spring fresh on Mr. Kinner's countenance, just as it had emerged on every teacher's face for the past several years of her schooling when they began to learn where she came from, what went into the making of a girl named Grace Picoletti.

***Available in softcover and e-book.***

Made in the USA
Monee, IL
03 October 2022